Pardon My French Press

J.P. Sterling

COFFEE LOFT
SERIES

Pardon My French Press

© copyright 2024 J.P. Sterling

Editors: Rebecca Carpenter, Brenda Bastien, Stained Glass Editing

This is a work of fiction. Any mention of names, places, and characters is fiction and for entertainment purposes only.

Not liable for any sudden coffee cravings which occur while reading this book.

Contents

To my friend, Peg, who has the best sense of humor, and always has a joke for me when I need one.

ONE
Christian Hanson

"I'm sorry, sir." The hotel receptionist clicks her ridiculously long and stabby nails on her desktop keyboard, glaring at me through her obviously fake eyelashes. "We don't have a reservation for a Christian Hanson, and we are fully booked for the night."

"Are you sure?" I shift my weight from one sneaker to the other while shuffling my worn leather backpack to the center of my back. My whole body aches from the most grueling commute ever. My flight from Boston to New York had been delayed, and eventually canceled, due to a winter storm. Of course, I only found that out after sitting at the airport for hours. I tried to rent a car. Any car would have done. I would have driven an electric scooter if

I had found one to rent. All the car rental companies were booked from the influx of flight cancellations.

But lucky me, I found a bus ticket. It should only have taken about five hours to get here, but with the reduced speeds from the road conditions, it took eight. I won't mention I had to sit by a gum-popping woman who didn't know the meaning of personal space. It had been a grueling day. All I wanted was my hotel room and a bed.

I let out a defeated sigh. In hindsight, the bus ticket was a good thing. It only set me back thirty-five bucks, which I didn't really have to spend anyway. A car would have been another dent on the credit card.

I don't doubt that I will pay it *someday*.

That someday due date is largely what contributes to the recent knot in my gut. I'm on a mission to make it smaller, not larger. It's all part of my plan to realize my dreams of true financial abundance. "I'm certain I booked a long stay. A whole month, in fact. Can you check under the name Christy? I know it's weird, but it's close to Christian and sometimes that happens."

Her eyes widen, fanning her spider-leg lashes. "Just one moment." More clickity clicks with her knife nails. "I'm sorry, Sir," her automatic not-sorry tone resumes. "We don't have a reservation for *Christy* Hanson. Last I checked, most of the hotels and shelters on the east side of the city are full, as they pulled homeless off the streets for the night. The weather forecast is for record lows tonight."

I rake my hand through my hair as tension pools in the back of my brain. I clearly recall making the reservation when I booked the flight. It is . . . well, maybe not clearly. I almost vaguely remember making the reservation. I pull out my phone, tap my emails, and scroll.

"Is there anything else I can help you with, Sir?" Spider lashes rushes me.

"Well, hmm, I'm looking for my confirmation number." I scroll, knowing the email is here. "Maybe you could try Christian *Manson*?"

Her lips tighten together, not even twitching as she resumes her clickity clicks, this time with more force. "I'm sorry, Sir—"

"You know," I hold up my palm, "it's fine. Thank you for your assistance. I'll call around to another hotel." I had heard her say all the hotels were full, but standing here is a waste of time. Tomorrow is a huge day, my first day at my Coffee Loft store. With the excitement brewing, my nerves twist into a tighter knot thinking about it.

My Coffee Loft is located in the middle of Station Square on Long Island, a historic building founded in 1906, with a Tudor roof resembling something straight out of Europe. It was a fantasy location, which I was lucky to be able to snag when a local coffee shop sold out.

I started working at a Coffee Loft franchise in college as a barista. I would have never dreamed that five years later I'd own my own. The Coffee Loft franchise has been good to me. I loved it so much. Now that I own my own store, it is fulfilling my dream of building an empire. Sure, it takes huge sacrifices right now. It's worth it to show my family, especially my grandma, everything I did on my own. She'd be proud of me. She might even smile as big as she used to before my mom passed.

I push off from the counter and roll my single suitcase back toward the exit, scrolling my phone for hotels. Nothing on this part of Long Island. Just as spider lashes said. Everything on the east side of New York is booked. I sure didn't have the funds to take a cab to Jersey, and I couldn't handle another bus. A brief glance from the lobby window shows thickening snowfall blowing at a near-horizontal slant.

I wish I had the money to secure a long-term Airbnb, but it might be a month or two of working before I have money to do that. I need somewhere to lay my head for a few hours until I can look for something nicer tomorrow.

I had carefully selected this hotel because it is the cheapest on Long Island, and it is only a block away from the Coffee Loft. My eyes arc around the top of my lids as an idea fills my brain. I mean, it is *my* store. It's a block away, and it would give me a respite for the night. It's not a Holiday Inn, but it's warm, has a bathroom, and a sofa I can crash on in my office . . .

I flash my phone screen, confirming it is nine. All the staff should be gone. It's not like anyone will even see me sleep there.

Why not?

I shove my phone into my coat pocket and head out the exit.

My feet crunch in the new layer of snow as the sidewalks are nearly empty—a rare scene for a city normally so bustling even at this time of night. I pull my wool jacket collar up, hugging it against the bottom of my ears, but it barely takes the sting off. I am not dressed for a winter walk. I pace faster, shoving my hands in my pockets to keep my fingers from freezing.

At the corner, I wait for the crossing light. It's too cold to stand still, so I shuffle my feet in place, trying to keep warm. Across the street is a small grocery store that's been closed for the night. A soft light glows in the window, displaying some of their bakery items.

A flitter of movement next to the building catches my eye.

A homeless man standing under the awning, with nothing more than a light jacket on. My first thought is to look away, and I check on the crossing light. Still red. My mind returns to spider lashes saying all the shelters and hotels are full for the night.

He'll freeze.

The subway exit is right behind him, and it gives me an idea as I reach in my fleece-lined pocket and pull out my wallet.

A few bucks cash, and my credit card.

The light finally swaps to green, and I cross the street, walking the cash over to him. With a weary smile, I offer it to him. "Do you think you can get on the subway with this to stay warm?"

His eyes grow softer when they catch mine. "God bless you."

"Don't mention it." I reach around his back, giving it a pat. "Stay safe."

"You too." He grabs his lone backpack by his foot, and shuffles away.

I pivot and marvel at the most magnificent building I've ever seen.

My Coffee Loft.

Two

Portia Grant

I ogle the open Coffee Loft pantry; all my morals are being tested.

One Oreo.

My favorite snack. The only thing better than an Oreo, is an Oreo with milk. Or ice cream. Yeah, an Oreo ice cream blended treat. You could add sprinkles on top, too . . . like for kids. I giggle to myself as I'm almost thirty and clearly past the age of sprinkles unless I *need* to eat them. Then I would. Like if someone put a gun to my head and growled, "eat these colorful sprinkle treats, or else." *Of course, I'm going to eat them in that situation.* Sprinkles are an option. For other people. A vibrantly colorful and delicious option.

My stomach churns ungracefully, reminiscent of those old-fashioned hand churned-ice-cream makers, but with the handle off kilter and in need of some fresh grease in the gears. It pains in the worst way, making a dying noise, reminding me of all the meals I didn't eat today.

We use Oreos in our blended drinks, and I opened this pack a few days ago. I eyeball the Oreo. One cookie isn't enough to make a drink. *Besides,* it's likely a tad stale. Not spoiled rotten, just approaching its use by date.

I'll have to throw it out in the morning.

I check over my shoulder, expecting someone to stop me. Of course, I am solo. Being short staffed today, I barista'd without a dinner break. A grumble erupted from my stomach, the call of a blue whale reverberating all around.

I eye the trash can in the corner, still overstuffed, waiting for me to tie the bag and take it out back. It didn't really have room for an Oreo.

I'd need a fresh trash bag for one lonely Oreo. That is wasteful. If I did put it in the trash, it might even attract rats. New York has a huge problem with rats, and I don't want to contribute to that. Would it really be stealing if it was going in the trash in the morning?

My fingers nearly tremble as I snatch it. Saliva musters at the tip of my tongue. Adrenaline surges, as I have never stolen anything in my life.

This obviously isn't stealing.

I nibble off the edge with my front teeth. *A tad soft on the outside, but mostly still crunchy.*

A childish giggle escapes from the back of my throat as I unscrew the two sides and scrape off the creamy filling with my teeth, melting it on my tongue. I relish every second of this drop of heaven. This cookie was a lot like me. The perfect metaphor to describe the state of my life. Although I had developed my first row of crows-feet in the corners of my eyes, I was in my prime on the inside. Not expired at all. Certainly, still worthy of a fairytale love story.

I replace the two halves together and bite the cookie, taking most of it into my mouth. Man, I'm starving. I hardly chew it. *So good.* My churning stomach screeches out for more.

Really, I deserve a free Oreo.

It is the least this place could do for me. I'd worked since noon without a break, which is *illegal*. But short staffed or not, I'm not about to let our customers down—I have too great of a work ethic for that even if I hate this place a little more each day.

This coffee house had always been a family-owned shop. Recently the owners retired, selling out to some new guy who is transitioning the store to a Coffee Loft franchise. At first, we were all excited, thinking we'd get big raises. Coffee Loft has the best coffees, but right after the sale went through, the jerk owner sent an email stating nobody was allowed to get more than twenty hours a week. That meant we had to work every shift by ourselves. He also said something about a new pay scale that would be applied after an in-person evaluation is completed. That didn't sound like big raises to me. Everyone except me, and one newer gal, Jade, had quit. They didn't want to have to prove they knew how to do a job they'd already been doing.

I'm confident in my abilities. Since I was the person running this place for the last year, he needs me. When everyone quit, he gave me special permission to work as much as I needed to until he gets here. Since I worked so hard, I should get a huge raise. Add in the corporate insurance, and it is too hard to say no—at least for right now.

I have goals. I'm not going to work here *forever*.

Because I really hate it here.

I ball my hand into a fist and pound on my chest, as I nearly choke on that scathing thought.

I can't even imagine the crow's feet I'd have after working this slave labor job forever, or even five more years. That's why I'm devoting all my free time to building my own match-making business. Sure, it's not making a profit *now*, but things take time. And until it takes off, I must put in the long hours here to be able to keep my apartment.

Nope. I'm only staying long enough to get my match-making business in the black. Another year, tops.

I shove the last of the Oreo into my mouth.

This part is mostly stale. It was only a little fresh on the outside. A façade to trick me into putting the whole thing in my mouth.

Fighting the reflex to gag, I stifle all thoughts of how the Oreo has instantly become a personification of everything wrong with my life. The underappreciated days of working here, ghosts of failed attempts to turn my life around—the latest being my app. And the fact that I always have been, and always will be single.

A shuffle from behind alerts me—my eyes pop open, and I stare at the growing shadow on the pantry wall straight in front of me.

A rather large shadow of a human figure.

My breath catches in my chest.

That's not *my* shadow!

My shadow is cute and petite. Never reflecting a pound over one twenty-five. Okay, maybe one forty-five, but I'm not a teenager anymore. Plus, I just wolfed down an Oreo! This shadow is much too shadowy to be one hundred and twenty-five—*okay, forty-five pounds*. It was more like two hundred with broody shoulders.

But I'm alone.

I had locked the front door, even pulling on the handle to double check it. I have had nightmares about this very moment. It always started the same. Me, a beautiful woman trapped alone here.

Which means . . .

Someone broke in!

My legs buckle while my adrenaline surges through my veins and all my senses are heightened.

I'm getting robbed!

"Are you eating company Oreos?" the shadow asked, not sounding the least bit concerned about my recent near-starving situation.

Oh no! My throat closes from panic, cinching my esophagus, and putting pressure on my airway. With my mouth still full, everything backed up. I can't breathe through my nose. I swallow the Oreo, but it isn't chewed enough. My hand flies to my throat as a gurgling noise crooks out.

This is bad!

I need water!

I stumble backward, gurgles crackling out of my throat as I bolt to the sink.

Where's a cup?

My eyes rapidly inventory the shined stainless-steel sink and counter. The bare counter sparkles with perfect shine from the cleanup I had recently completed. Not one single stray cup. I do spot my French press in the center of the counter. *That's going to have to do!*

I gurgle again. It's not an attractive sound at all. Feet shuffle behind me, and the voice calls out, "Are you choking?" I wish with *everything in my soul* I could answer that with a giant sarcastic, *no,* but I can't force out even a peep.

Now woozy, I need to do something! Panicking, I spin on my heel and flail forward.

A set of strong arms swoops in from behind. Hands lock below my ribcage. My last breath wrings out of my lungs like a dish rag twisting. I was either being attacked or Heimliched. With no breath left inside of me to fight, my body goes limp.

My ribs crackle from a gut punch. I'm still unsure if this is an attack, or the Heimlich.

Never had either.

A puff of air, I didn't even know I had, rushes out of my lungs with enough force that I cough. My Oreo heaves out.

Hallelujah, I'm alive! I inhale deep breaths, falling to my knees to aid the process as I hold my chest.

I nearly died.

How's that for karma for stealing?

I'm never doing that again!

But I'm rescued by this perfect stranger sent to me.

Is he an angel?

A paranormal paramedic of some sort?

I rub my throat as I continue to draw in air, catching my bearings. I slowly raise my head. I must know who he is.

My jaw drops as he's *gorgeous*.

Not just a little gorgeous, but I've never seen anything like him.

A steaming cup of hot cocoa hot! The narrator's voice in my head doesn't shut up, tracking all his most impressive features. A chiseled jaw line dominates his face in all the best ways. Dark hair with a rebellious front spike, most likely caused by an unruly cowlick, but he wears it well. Eyes a perfect hue of blue, wavering from the colors of deep-sea water all the way over to light gray.

Fascinating.

Who is he?

Unbidden goosebumps dot my spine, and I pinch my brows together as I ask the first thing that bleeps out, "Are you robbing me?"

THREE

Christian

My heart rate tames as I place my hand firmly on her back. My insides freeze, and I hold my breath. I've never been good in emergency situations—which is why I went into the coffee business—not first response. "Just relax." I focus on measured breathing, taking my own advice. "You're okay."

She stands with her hand propped on the counter, wearing a Coffee Loft apron. She's clearly an employee, but the fact that she's here hours past closing is confusing. Her blonde hair is tied up in one of those disheveled buns that oddly looks put together, accentuating her high cheekbones. As her breath evens, her gaze shifts to me. Her eyes are colored like wild July-sun-ripened blueberries so electrifyingly beautiful they vortex me right in. There's a magnetism that's instant.

Shuffling her feet backwards, she adds distance between us. "Are you robbing me?"

I burst out laughing as my head springs back. "No, I'm not robbing you." Pausing, I consider how strange my being here might look. It was hours past closing time, and I had to look like a homeless person lugging my suitcase. Yet, she was the one eating *my* Oreos when I walked in. I can forgive one cookie, but I'm going to give her a hard time with it. I point a finger gun at her, lightening the mood. "It looks like you were robbing me."

"What?" Her T is extra sharp. Clearly, she got her breath back. She eases along the wall, lifting the fire extinguisher from its hook, and aims the nozzle at me with her hand secured on the trigger. "What are you doing here? And you better speak fast before I call the cops."

"Whoa." I throw my hands up as if I'm under arrest. "I'm Christian, the new owner. I didn't break in; I have a key." I emit another series of chuckles as she can't be serious.

"Wait." Her eyes shift side to side before locking on me. "You're the new owner?"

"I am." My lips twist into a grin which I hope convinces her not to soak me.

Her hand flops forward, and she drops the fire extinguisher to the tile as she emits an explosive sigh. "Why didn't you say something instead of sneaking up on me like that. You nearly killed me!"

"Me?" Jabbing my thumb into my chest, I connect the pattern where she shifts the blame to me, and my defensive senses rise all the way to my neck. "I saved you! You were choking. If I hadn't performed that heroic life-saving maneuver, you'd be toast." I guffaw in disgust. "You should be thanking me."

"Thank you?" Her jaw drops and she makes a face as if she's going to vomit. This woman was clearly not in control of her bodily functions. Nearly choking to death, and now dry heaving, all in the span of five whole minutes. Not sure what that suggests.

Maybe she needs a chiropractic adjustment?

Laughter rushes out, her breath is warm as a summer breeze as a wave of it meets my nose. It also smells like Oreos. "What's so funny?" I ask. She swipes at her eyes, wiping tears, with continued waves of laughter. This woman is clearly unhinged. It's a good thing I caught her eating my Oreos now, or who knows what she would have stolen from me. "Ma'am—"

Her laughter drops off, and she deploys an accusing finger at me. An extra pointy digit, with a not-even-close-to-conversational slant at my mouth. "Don't ma'am me."

Sweat beads on my forehead. Why do I feel as if I'm breaking the law in my own business? "I'm so confused right now. Why am I the one in trouble?"

"You snuck up on me, tried to kill me, had the audacity to accuse me of stealing, and you called me ma'am."

"But you are okay now, right?" I force an even tone, trying to infuse a calmer environment. "Or should I call a paramedic?"

"I'm fine." She crosses her arms over her chest, and sharply angles her hip away from me. "That's not the point."

"What is the point?" I ask softly, lowering my voice even more, as I see my moderated voice is bringing down her anxiety. "What are we arguing about?"

Her brow dips into a low V, and she emits a huff so quiet it is barely audible. "You are saying what?"

"Nothing really." My shoulders fall, releasing tension as we are finally about ready to have a normal conversation. "Maybe that I'm Christian, your new boss." I throw out my hand, offering a handshake. "Nice to meet you. I'm glad you lived. What did you say your name was?"

Her chin raises, and she receives my hand, her skin is smooth as Ivory soap. "Portia. I'm the one you spoke with over email. Everyone but me, and one other gal, quit."

I bobble my head a few times as this isn't exactly pleasurable news. Apparently, she is one of my only trained staff. If I want to keep this place going without closing, I'll need her. At least until I hire and train someone else. It is the week before Christmas, though, and adding new staff now would be impossible. Better to be nice to her. "Thank you," I manage through my racing thoughts as my to-do list continues to stack up in my brain. I hadn't planned on needing to hire and train a whole new staff. Training can be costly, and I don't have any spare funds.

She triple blinks. "You're welcome." Her words are quick, mirroring a child who was being forced to have manners.

"Now that we established you lived," I scan the room, everything appearing to be in its place, except for the fact she is here hours after closing, "is there a reason you're here. Do you need a ride?"

A sigh rumbles in her throat before she finally pushes it out with force. "I'm here because I am working. It took me forever to clean since I was by myself all day."

"Okay." I chain nod about six times, as this reminds me of talking to my little sister. The attitude. "Well, I appreciate that. I'm here now and can finish up." I want to say, will you leave so I can sleep, but that won't win me any respect.

"I did everything, but you're welcome to inspect if you think it needs it." She paces to the employee coatroom, calling back, "I haven't had a day off in three weeks. Would you mind me taking the weekend off?"

Now it is my turn to nearly choke, as she springs back out of the coatroom and beelines to the door. Of course, I never expected anyone to work three weeks without a day off. I didn't know this place had been so depleted on staff, or I would have just shut the door completely until I got here. In our email correspondence, she always sounded as if everything was fine. The knot in my throat swells another notch as overwhelm consumes me. I had no idea I'd have this much immediate stress. "I'll handle it," I grumble.

Four

Portia

In my tenth-floor studio apartment, I lie on my second-hand futon with a white, goose-feather down comforter pulled over my face, blocking the burst of sunlight coming in from the bottom of my cracked open window. I could easily reach over and close it, but I'm too lazy to do that.

Plus, I don't have control over the heat in my place. It's an old system, and only the building manager has temp controls. Once he cranks the boiler on for the year, all the heat rises to the top floor. The bottom floor people complain about freezing all winter, while the top floor roasts in smoldering heat. Even though it's December on Long Island, if I leave my window closed it will rise to almost eighty degrees. It's a good thing my gas bill is included in my rent, or I'd be looking for a different apartment.

I yawn, pulling the pillow over my head to darken the room more. Finally, a day off! A text bleeps on my phone. There's no way I can answer that.

Another text. Still not answering that.

I adjust the pillow to cover my ears.

And another one.

This better be an emergency, or I will quickly make it one.

I snake my arm out of the covers, and grapple for the phone on my nightstand slash end table. I don't even have the screen to my face yet, and it vibrates with another text. One eye peels open.

Jade: Did you know the new owner is here? I came in a few minutes late this morning, expecting it to be you, and it was him. He's all over my case about my clock-in times.

Jade: Why are you not here? You didn't quit, did you? Please don't quit. I can't afford to quit, too.

Jade: I don't like him.

Jade: He bobbles his head when he talks.

I stretch my hands way over my head and arch my back, setting off a chain reaction as my cat, Mr. Noodles, joins me in our morning cat stretch. This used to be the most joyful part of my day, snuggling with Mr. Noodles. Today, I had to tend to this. I grumble, flop over onto my back, hover my phone over my face, and type.

Me: I met him last night. Sorry, it was so late that I forgot to warn you.

Jade: He has some sort of OCD or something because he's literally doing inventory on everything. Instead of helping me make drinks, he is counting Oreos. It's so weird.

A snort blurts out of my lips, and I can't help but take pride in that. Mr. Noodles paws at my arm, signaling it is time to fill his bowl. I drop my phone on my comforter and get up, not taking a moment to straighten my bed. I have zero plans to make my bed today. After I get some food, it's back to bed with my laptop to do admin work for my match-making business. Heaven!

Well, the bed part is heaven. The work part is okay. I love my little matching business, but it turns out it's harder to make a profit than I thought. To funnel people into the site, I give them a free match. Clients are meeting partners and dropping off the site at record speeds before they even sign up for a paid membership-hence why I am not making money. I'm in major need of recruiting new people. That I can't do from my bed.

Since I'm at emergency lows with potential dates on my website, I say sure when my dad calls around noon to ask if I want to go to Home Hardware. Dad is a retired carpenter with a lower back to prove it. He doesn't do much handyman stuff anymore, but he claims to miss the ambiance of the hardware store. Saturday outings are a regular thing for us. I tend to think it isn't so much about the ambiance as it is his need to get out of the house. It is evident that my parents still love each other after nearly forty years of marriage, but it is no secret that retirement is bringing them a little *too* close together.

My mom used to enjoy her days doing craft projects and quilting. If you had come home in the middle of the day, the kitchen table would be covered in whatever she was working on. Now that Dad is home, he sits at the table and plays online racing games on his tablet. I don't see the harm in it. He could do a lot worse things, but Mom says the fake engine noise gets on her nerves. I guess I can understand that.

Back to Home Hardware, I'm terrified of anything sharp and can't lift a thing over thirty pounds, but it turns out it has another product I need. The store is loaded with hunks. Dad knows how headstrong I am. He has long since given up arguing with me, instead insisting he come with me. Nobody can say my dad doesn't support me.

While Dad spends an hour talking about the weather to the guy in the paint aisle, I push the cart up the light bulb aisle and scout each guy I pass. Wedding ring. Wedding ring. No Wedding ring. Also no teeth. Oh, no wedding ring and a full set of teeth! I nonchalantly cut in front of him, reach for something on the shelf above my head, and wiggle my fingers, signaling I can't get it.

"Let me help you with that." He falls for my plan, rushing to my aid. "I got it." His fingers brush against the LED light bulbs, a pack of eight. "Is this the right one?"

Since I only have two fixtures in my entire studio, I have no clue what I will do with all these lightbulbs. The branding on the side of the box says, "Each bulb lasts twenty years." I quickly compute the math. If I live in my two-fixture studio forever, that pack of bulbs will last me for the next hundred and twenty years! I couldn't back down on my plan now. "Yes, that's exactly the one I need. Thank you." I take the box from him and place it neatly in the corner of the cart. Then I raise my lashes back to him and sweetly say, "I bet your girlfriend appreciates how tall you are?"

He adopts a flirty smile, picking up on my banter. "No girlfriend. I actually just got back from a military deployment."

"That's amazing. Thank you so much for your service." Batting my lashes again, I slide a QR code card out of my purse. "You know, I don't normally do this, but I have a match-making business. It's very exclusive. I have a waiting list, but I'm overcome with such an appreciation for your kindness. I would love to offer you a free match. Will you accept this code?" I smile, hoping he can't tell I'm lying through my teeth. Not only do I not have a waiting list, I also only have four available female matches currently.

His gaze slides to my card, and he smiles a little suspiciously. "Matchmaking?"

"Yeah, it's called, Your Last First Date. It differs from other dating sites because it focuses on personality matches. There are no profile photos until you unlock that feature. You don't get a name until after you chat with someone. It's a lot of fun." I pull my lips into the tightest grin I can. "It's the least I could do to thank you for your service." I cross my toes. I'm not a contortionist, it's clearly a saying meaning I cinch my toes together. Waiting.

"How do you match people without letting people select?"

"I love that question." I run a hand through my long hair, tucking it behind my ears. "I have a series of required personal questions. If you want, you can go into further personality quizzes, things that take your Myers-Briggs category into consideration. Then the algorithm does the rest. It's a lot of fun."

He takes the card from me. "My name is Liam, by the way."

Of course, his name is Liam! Every hot, single guy on this side of the Brooklyn bridge is always Liam. He's so perfect for my site. I can't wait for him to meet his dream girl. "I'm Portia. Nice to meet you, Liam." I hold my grin, backing away with my one hundred-and-twenty-year-light supply and steer my cart back toward my dad while I wave. "Well, I better let you continue your day. Thanks again."

Now, to find some more women for my site. With Liam as bait, it shouldn't be a problem. I need to leave Home Hardware for the ladies, though.

I round the corner, nearly crashing into Dad. His gaze slides to my one-hundred-and-twenty-year supply of lights, and a proud dad smile lands on his lips. "Ah, you caught one, huh?" The first time I recruited with him, I thought it would be cringe. It turns out he viewed it like fishing, and kept score for me, too.

"Military, and very polite."

"That's not too bad." He sneaks a look at his drugstore wristwatch. The leather strap has long been worn out, but somehow, he keeps it together by punching new holes in it each time it snaps. I swear he's had that watch since I was five. Being an all-around handyman, he doesn't believe in throwing anything out that can be fixed. "It's not even one o'clock yet. You have time to get another one. Do you want to cruise the car lot?"

A smile glues to my lips because Dad's the kind of dad who'll do anything for me, and clearly *does* do most things for me. "I don't know if I can handle the car lot with you today." That's the one place I have to keep an eye on him, as he might come home with something he's not supposed to. He's always had a passion for cars—hence the name Portia. "Nah, I'm not a fan of the car lot men. I might see if I can borrow Mrs. Nelson's dog again later, and pretend to lose him at the park. She's been letting me walk him since the elevator broke. It worked well last time. The guys at the park tend to be fit and outgoing, matching the fastest."

"You know, Portia." Dad places a hand on the cart handle, slowing it down as I turn and catch his gaze. His blue eyes match mine. They haven't clouded even a spec over the years, still holding that same mischievous spark that used to take me on all the adventures when I was a kid. "One of these days, you might catch a hunk for you to keep."

"You know what I always say, Dad. Always a matchmaker, never a match." I sigh, wistfully. I'm not embarrassed to talk about my dating life. Mostly because there isn't anything to talk about. Plus, my dad is the easiest person to talk to about anything. Although I would never admit it, I would love to meet my own match. I force a smile, hoping he can't see the worry cloud my eyes.

One of my greatest fears in life is living my whole life in auto mode, working a job I don't have a passion for, doing the same routine without feeling anything and without finding my true love. I want to find love, but I'm also building a dream. It's a hard balance to juggle. At least for right now, I'm fine pouring my heart into this app while I wait for my last first date.

Besides, if I have a boyfriend, he won't be okay with my cruising for dudes with my dad, and this seriously is the most fun I've had. I know my dad would miss it as much as I would. Then we'd have to find a new hobby together. Something like real fishing, and fish are stinky.

Five

Christian

"What happened to my French press?" Portia stands on her toes, peering into the top cupboard. "I always leave it on the counter next to the espresso machine, and it's gone."

"I threw it away." I loiter in front of the microwave, nuking my left-over takeout pasta from last night. The same takeout pasta I've had *every* night for the last week since I arrived here. I don't love pasta. In fact, I'm getting sick of it. The mere smell of the cheese makes my stomach curdle, but it comes in a box from the neighboring grocery store for super cheap. Anything I can do to save a dollar is worth it. I don't doubt I'll be on a noodles and air diet for weeks—if not months—at the rate business is going.

Slowly she pivots and locks her gaze on me. "Why would you do that?"

"Coffee Loft doesn't sell French press coffee. We sell gourmet espresso at top shelf prices."

"I wasn't going to make one to sell. That's what I prefer to drink." She shuts the cupboard, and parks one hand on her hip. "You could have asked before you threw it away. That was *my* personal French press."

"I'm sorry I didn't realize you left personal belongings laying around." I shrug, knowing this transition is going to be hard for her. "I thought it belonged to the previous owner, and since I bought this place, it would be mine."

Her eyes pace to the pantry, and back to the ingredient canisters on the counter. "Did you also throw all the Oreos away because I can't find those anywhere?"

"Ah, we must be out." I wince, pretending not to care, as it doesn't make sense to tell an Oreo thief where I hide the Oreos. The microwave dings. I grab my pasta, and head back to my office. In the rush to open the shop this morning alone—because Jade was late again—I had no time to eat until now. Jade couldn't have caught me at a worse moment.

I'm not proud of what I did. When she came in late, I was so overwhelmed, I ended up letting her go. Jade was never on time, and you'd think for having a new boss, you'd at least try. Sure, today is Christmas Eve, and terrible timing, but she'd need to go eventually with her performance. I might as well give her the holiday off.

I'm not a jerk.

The stress added up too fast.

Now, there's this constant constriction in my chest, and I'm having trouble breathing. I still haven't found a hotel that doesn't cost a kidney. I finally got a rental car dropped off, which gives me more options for a hotel. As soon as I have time, I'm going online to book a room. It had been a week since I had slept in an actual bed, and it is wearing on my mental health. Not to mention the kink in my neck.

That wasn't even the worst pain I had. It turns out the previous owners didn't provide accurate records. I had requested three years of tax returns at the time of closing. Now that I can see the actual sales, it is clear they were fudging the numbers to prepare it for sale. There is no way they were making the kind of money they said they were banking. Either that, or all their customers left when they sold the place. Sometimes that happens. Customer loyalty is a real thing.

There is the typical morning rush you'd expect for a coffee shop, but that only lasts an hour, or so, and it quickly dies down to nothing but a slow drip of random people throughout the day. There is no reason we'd ever need two people working simultaneously. Not to mention the bad habits of the two people I had. Plus, they were both being paid inflated management wages. I don't need management anymore. I need cheap labor. There's no way they'd stand for a pay cut. I know I wouldn't.

I'm coming to terms with what needs to be done. I hate this situation, but it's better to let my overpaid management go. They can draw unemployment. I can regroup with new people. After the holidays, I'll have a huge grand reopening ceremony to introduce the Coffee Loft brand.

I shovel pasta into my mouth and stare at the deposit slip I filled out. Twenty-three bucks and eighteen cents. Not worth even going to the bank. Sure, most people pay with plastic or digital these days, but even that won't keep this place running. I must assume the old owners used this place as a tax write-off of some sort, but I can't do that. I'll lose everything. I barely got financing for this place. If it wasn't for my grandma putting up her own business as collateral to obtain a personal loan, I wouldn't even be sitting here.

No, I don't need to go to the bank, but I'm going to walk there anyway for some fresh air and a chance to clear my head. I shove the deposit slip in my pocket and emerge from the office to find Portia leaning over the counter with a coffee cup in one hand and a Sharpie in the other. Her hair is pulled up into twin messy buns, and her smile is bright and inviting. Despite all the sass, she really is beautiful. "So, you said your first name is Brad?" She writes the customer's name on the cup. That part I don't have a problem with. It's what spews out of her mouth next that makes my mocha boil. "Tell me, Brad. Are you getting a drink for your girlfriend, or is it just—"

"That's enough!" I step in front of her and steal the cup. My blood pressure spikes, and I remind myself to take deep breaths. "Stop hitting on the customers," I grumble as I place the cup next to the espresso machine while I run shots.

"I wasn't *hitting* on him," she hisses under her breath. "I'm trying to find out if he's single."

"I don't care if you were buying him a winning lottery ticket," I hiss. "It's not appropriate to harass the customers like that." I empty the espresso shots into the cup and seal the lid before handing the cup to Brad. Portia and I watch silently as Brad leaves, but as soon as the door closes behind him, we resume the same fight we've been having since she came in at noon. "You need to start being professional, or—"

"Or what?" She parks her hand haughtily on her perfectly rounded hip. "Go ahead and tell me that I'm getting fired, because I'd really like to see you run this place without me."

"Don't even test me. I already let Jade go this morning."

"What? You let Jade go?" Her jaw unhinges, flapping all the way down until I can see the dental filling in her lower left side. It's nothing disgusting but hints of a sweet tooth. "You're bluffing. Why would you do that?"

I toss a shoulder up into an *I'm-bored-of-this-conversa-tion* shrug. "It wasn't anything personal. I reworked the budget, and I need to revamp things to save money. She was paid management wages, and I don't need a manager as I'm here. Add to it, the fact she's been late every day for the last two weeks."

"You weren't even here the last two weeks. You have no idea how hard we've been working." Her eyes narrow until there is nothing left but tiny slits. "You are a jerk."

"That almost sounds like disrespecting your boss." My words were low, hinting at a warning. Judging from the looks of the books, I had to assume that Jade and Portia had been running this place into the ground, and I don't feel bad about needing to take this place in a new direction. A direction that makes money. It's not personal. Well, a little personal because I really didn't care for her sass, but it is also business.

"Go head, and fire me," she huffs as she juts out her chin. "You wouldn't last one week without me. You'd lose all your business. Nobody is going to buy coffee from your bobble head."

"Oh, really?" My head tilts, partially from the kink in my neck, but even more than that, it's what happens when my ego weighs in. It's a minor flaw that happens sometimes. "Not only will I 'handle' it by myself without you and Jade," I insert finger quotes around the word handle. I'm so worked up from the stress of everything, I'm acting completely out of character by feeding into her attitude, "It'll be my best week ever."

Her voice drops so low, it's hardly above a whisper. "What are you saying?"

My lips twist into a sinister grin. Maybe from the stress of sleeping on an ancient sofa that smells like sweaty feet. Maybe it's ego. Something gets into me. "I'm saying you can leave. I don't need your attitude. I certainly don't want to keep my Oreos on lockdown anymore."

"Well." Portia sticks her leg out, tapping her foot as if it is helping her to keep from running her mouth. "Just you wait, and you'll see I'm right. You'll come crawling back."

"Doubt it." I nod to the door. "Leave your apron, and I'll send your check in the mail."

"You're serious?" She whips off her apron and balls it up. I duck, assuming she's going to hurl it at me, but she maintains her composure and stuffs it in the hamper on her way out. "Just wait until I tell everyone you painted over black mold!"

"You can't do that!" I yell, pacing after her toward the exit. "That's slander!" I doubt she hears me, because the door is already shut. I brush my hands together, feeling a job well done. Problem number two is solved. Now that I don't have her harassing my customers, I'll surely get *way* more business. I can focus on my grand reopening, and everything is going to be amazing from here on out.

I scan the empty foyer, tracing the unfilled aisle to the counter. Nothing but emptiness. The clock ticks loudly on the wall behind me, and for the first time since I've been here, I notice a hum from the light in the dessert display case. I walk back to the office, yank out a sheet of printer paper, and scribble Help Wanted. When I come back to tape it in the window, I scan up and down the street. Empty. "It *is* Christmas Eve. People are with their families. Just give it a couple of days until people realize this place has a hip new owner, and a fresh look." I tell myself. "Then it'll be packed."

Six

Portia

"Dad," I huff through the phone as I steer Mrs. Nelson's English Mastiff through the jogging path in Central Park. Well, actually one look at the size ratio and you'll know who is steering who. The size differential is what makes this recruiting endeavor so fruitful. "I got fired from the coffee shop."

"You did?" The lack of shock in his voice tips me off that he was expecting something like this. "Were you recruiting on your shift again?"

"That's not the point." I yank the leash to the side of the path, pulling Oliver into the grass while we pass a trio of Shih Tzus. Oliver is smart, excellent at following directions, but he never understands his size. He wants to play with everyone, often scaring away every breed smaller than him. "The point is that Christian is a jerk. And he threw out my French press. He had the audacity to say I was hurting his business, and he'd be better off without me."

"I don't know about that. You've got the best sales skills I've ever seen." Dad's even voice was laced with a chuckle. "It's a bit of a cliché, but you could sell ice to an Eskimo. When you put your mind to something, you go after it."

"Exactly." I tug on the leash again, directing Oliver away from the hot dog cart. I'm not against feeding him street food, but I usually reserved such treats for a reward after he brings me a hunk.

"So, what are you doing now?" His voice takes an inquiring tone. "Is the app making any money?"

"That's the thing." I halt on my heel as I pass a single jogger with no wedding band. A look over my shoulder confirms he's fit and definitely fast enough to run after Oliver. I cradle the phone between my ear and shoulder as I use both hands to unhook Oliver's leash, while discreetly pointing to the man jogging away. "That's the one we want, boy. When I say go." Oliver dances in place, doing his I-found-a-hunk-excited-tail wag while I pause, letting the jogger get a good length away.

This works best when it looks as if I don't have a chance to catch Oliver. While I wait, I continue my conversation with Dad. "The app's algorithm is successful. Which sounds like a good thing, and typically it is, but I can't keep people long enough for a second date. With the first one free, it's like one date and they're off to happily ever after. It never fails. A perfect match every time."

"That's amazing the algorithm works that well."

"Not really, because I got most of my female recruits from the coffee shop. Now that I can't go there daily, I'm not sure how I will keep up with the supply."

"Who said you can't go there every day? He doesn't own the whole block."

"What are you saying? Just recruit on Christian's doorstep." My voice trails off. That is the *perfect* idea. It would also annoy him like crazy, and I'm all for that. I'll have to think about that another time. My hunk is a good quarter mile away. It is time to put my plan into action. "Gotta go, Dad. I've got a hunk to catch." I hang up before I give Dad a chance to reply. I point toward the man and instruct Oliver. "Fetch!"

Oliver bolts forward with lightning speed. I grab my foot and pull it behind my leg, stretching. It's been a while since we'd been hunting in the park, and I need to limber up. I grab the other foot and give it a good tug as Oliver rounds the corner on the jogging path. He's about halfway between the man and me now, and I start a slow jog to warm up some more. When Oliver's about to pass the man and not a moment too soon, I call out, "Oliver! Come back!"

I dig in and pull speed, running as if my life depends on it, and scream for help. "Somebody, please stop my dog!"

The shrillness in my cries for help even startles me. I had this routine down to a science, and as I'd hypothesized, this man is fast. He jolts forward, taking a mere ten seconds to snatch Oliver by the collar. Now is not the time to stop crying. I learned it is best to carry on a little longer while I worked up a few crocodile tears. "Oliver!" I cry out. "Why do you do this to me?"

The man holds Oliver's collar, jogging him toward me. I continue my script, "Ah, thank you so much! I'm not sure how he got off his leash." I grab Oliver's collar and hook his leash while scratching his head with my free hand. Now that I am this close to our catch, I can see he's definitely a ten. He's over six feet, fit and could mirror Patrick Dempsey when he was younger. "I don't know what I would have done if you weren't here." I bat my lashes and smile at him sweetly. "He's not even my dog. I'm walking him for my neighbor. Your *girlfriend* must be lucky to have such a dashing and quick man around."

"I don't have a girlfriend." His lips curl up, ready to banter.

My smile curls even more. *I hooked another one.* I pat Oliver's head and quietly promise to get him a hotdog on the way home.

Now, to figure out what to do about losing my best recruiting spot.

Seven

Christian

It's the day after Christmas. I spent yesterday alone in my hotel room, finally resting in an actual bed. It might have been depressing to some people, but a real bed is the best Christmas present I could have had. I slept the day away, not even missing a big family gathering.

Today, I drum my fingers on the Coffee Loft counter, staring at my grandmother's name in my phone contact list. Even though she hated the idea of me buying this place, my grandma made a personal loan to me for it. She didn't give me any special privileges though. I had a strict loan repayment plan with an interest rate that was in her favor. My first loan payment is due next month, leaving me hardly any time to make money to pay her.

The store's low sales weren't the situation I had planned on. I also never planned on starting over with staff either. Although I do believe it's the best choice going forward, it's taking time to become profitable.

My grandma is wealthy. She mostly gets her wealth from real estate investments, but she also owns the construction business that my late grandfather spent his life building. Not a prestigious luxury home-building one, rather a dirty road construction company with big noisy trucks, of which she is so proud.

From the time I was a baby, they had me in a hard-hat, sitting in the dump truck next to Grandpa. They did everything they could to train me in the ways of a "blue-collar, working man." I always loathed it. I had allergies, and the filth and dust would make my eyes crust over and my nose plug up. I never complained, though, because passion oozed out of their smiles.

Grandma had held onto the dream that *someday* I would carry on their business for the next generation. She would have handed it over to me on a silver platter, complete with a ribbon-cutting ceremony. It's all I remember her talking to me about when I was little. "Someday, you will own Total Trucks Construction, and you can drive any truck you want." I never admitted it, but I merely pretended to enjoy playing with trucks when I was little, to see their pride shine.

My grandma even sent me to one of the best business schools in the country to get a formal education. For that, I'm grateful, and will never forget her gift. I didn't use it the way she had hoped. It's an understatement to say I broke Grandma's heart when I asked her for a loan for my Coffee Loft franchise. She gave me the loan papers with white knuckles.

I hope in time, after she sees my success, she will see this is a better fit for me.

More than that, I strive to make her proud.

Unfortunately, my timeline isn't working the way I need it to. I put the cart before the horse on a few things. A colossal cart that won't budge. I worked all morning and only four people came in. One didn't even order a drink, but asked to use the restroom. I don't doubt that Coffee Loft as a franchise has the tools it needs to help me turn this location around, but it could take time.

Time is expensive. I won't have the money to pay Grandma this month, but I don't want her to think I'm using her. I need to explain the situation now, so she isn't upset with me.

I drop my forehead into my palms and rub at the tension that's been there all week. No amount of peppermint mocha will help.

I'm out of options.

I press on my grandmother's number and hold my breath, counting the rings. One. Two. This won't take long. My grandmother sits next to her phone. If anything, she is probably playing Candy Crush on it. She has been a loyal addict of that game—and only that game—since it was first introduced. She must be on level one million by now. I count rings until it goes to voicemail. My insides freeze. She ignored my call. Then my internal organs add another layer of ice.

What am I going to do? She's going to think I blew her off and took advantage of her if I don't pay her.

I rake my fingers through my hair. I already paid an enormous amount of money to have mailers sent out to people in the neighborhood for free promo drinks next week. I've got commercials running, and radio ads booked. Short of begging on the street for people to come in, I don't know what to do to drive up business. It takes time for word to get out that this isn't the same old run-down coffee place it was.

How does this place have literally no customers?

For the first time, my denial wanes, and now anger bubbles in my gut.

Is the road blocked off?

Something is up.

I furrow my brow and stride to the door. Something must be going on in town to take all the people. A concert or a holiday parade. That must be it. I'm too new to town. I didn't even think to look at the schedule of events.

I place my hands on the glass door, gazing down the street. Traffic. Pretty boisterous, if you ask me. Why is nobody stopping in? My sign says open. I even double-check it, flipping it to closed and back again.

I turn my head to check the other direction. What I see startles me so much that my eyes immediately swell and bug out of my head, while my brain sets off a countdown to an explosion.

My hands ball into fists, and I struggle not to slam my hand through the glass. *I'm about to flip my froth,* but I don't need a repair bill.

Portia—my annoying ex-employee—is standing right outside my door. Her cheeks are rosy from the icy air, but she's bundled up in a heavy winter coat with a red and white striped scarf around her neck. Aside from the fact that she looks more festively beautiful than any actress in a Christmas movie, I can't stand to look at her. She is holding a French press by the handle, drinking coffee straight from it through a loopy straw!

Clearly, she is doing it to taunt me.

Was she serious about telling people I have mold?

She's running off all my customers!

This must be illegal.

It's clearly not ethical.

It's sabotage!

My brain flashes to her saying I wouldn't last a week without her. Now I know her plan.

She's unhinged! Like an oversized barn door flapping in the wind, teasing for the next giant windstorm where it goes flying out to kill someone. She's dangerous!

She's getting revenge on me for firing her. *Oh.* I rub my hands together, working up my own plan. Something to steal her—or rather MY—customers back.

It must be fast.

It has to be cheap.

I don't have time to waste. I'm bleeding money, and she is lying to all my customers.

I rub my temples as I think of a way to stop it.

I've got it!

I clamp down on my bottom lip, fighting with every ounce of my soul not to burst into laughter. Christian is pacing back and forth in front of the huge Coffee Loft window, and if looks could kill. Ah, my stomach wrenches from holding in my giggles.

I should not be this joyful, but it's the day after Christmas and is my best recruiting morning ever. I've handed out hundreds of QR cards this morning, and I already got a full baker's dozen of recruits into my apps. I've been so happy all day, I shimmy when I walk.

Dad never disappoints me, giving me a brand-new French press in my stocking yesterday. I'm so happy to see it, I'm drinking coffee straight from it. Of course, there's no coffee grounds in it. That would be weird. Dad bought coffee from the shop down the street, as I'm not going to patronize Christian. I giggled when Dad passed over my favorite childhood loppy straw, and I couldn't resist. I may look completely looney drinking coffee from a loopy straw, but I'm happy.

It didn't surprise me that Dad stayed to help. He rolls his eyes at my recruiting, but he's secretly proud of me. I couldn't have a better partner in crime. Not only does he not flinch when I recruit, but he's always a source of motivation. He reaches forward, offering help. "Give me a stack of QR codes."

Before I can answer, Christian whips open the Coffee Loft door and wails in protest, "Oh, no, you don't!" Christian pokes a slanted finger at me. "You're not standing here. It's private property."

I'm in such a good mood that not even Christian can ruin it. His previously bright blue eyes were wavering toward gray now, hinting at sadness. I tilt my head, inspecting them from a different angle.

Maybe not sad.

More stress and exhaustion.

Do I feel sorry for him?

NOPE. He fired me on Christmas Eve.

I stride closer to the street, making sure my shoulders are back. The sun is at high noon, making it brighter than usual, but something catches my eye. I squint, catch my breath. Before my heart sinks, I straighten my spine and develop a plan. Who does Christian really think he's up against?

I'm great with people.

All people.

Including this handsome police officer he's obviously called on me. Christian is still lurking in the shadows under the Coffee Loft canopy when the officer approaches. "Good morning, Officer," I bat my eyelashes. "Lovely day for a walk, isn't it?"

Christian snorts so loudly it draws the officer's sideways gaze. He must have felt the heat of the officer's stare, because he immediately goes on the defensive, blurting out, "Officer, she must be breaking some code. She's right in front of my business, bothering all my customers."

"It's not against the law for someone to walk." He motions down the sidewalk. "However, if you loiter, and harass citizens, that's an issue, and that's the report I've been given."

"Ah, no, sir." I widely wag my head back and forth, maintaining my innocence. "I'm simply enjoying the fresh air, but if it's a bother, I'll be on my way."

"That might be best." The officer's gaze drops to my giant coffee with the loopy straw, and the cards I'm clutching, but he doesn't ask about them. "You seem to be having a nice day. Maybe avoid this area if you can. You don't look like you're here, causing trouble."

Christian emits one of those screeches that's meant to be explosive, but he obviously suppresses it, leaving his face to flush a deep crimson as he runs back into the Coffee Loft. I pinch my side hard to stop cracking into laughter in front of the cop. I don't want him to get even a hint that this was anything more than a coincidence of location. "Thank you for your assistance."

"Absolutely." The officer takes a slow step away, and I call back with an air of flirtation while jerking my thumb over my shoulder at my dad, "Don't worry about me. Dad keeps me out of trouble."

He nods goodbye at my dad, then smiles one of those flirty sideways smiles at me before he turns around to leave. I'm giddy as I quickly turn back to my dad, who is lurking behind me. The fact that he's vouching for me to police officers warms my heart more than anything. No daughter on the planet has as much support as I do. Getting fired is stressful enough, but thanks to my dad who developed this plan, it turned into the most successful recruiting event.

Dad shoves his hand in his jacket pocket. "Well, honey, it might be best to move across the road for now."

I eye the business across the street. A family-owned pizzeria. I don't eat there often. They have excellent pizza, and the family is one of the sweetest in the area. They wouldn't mind me there, but I only have the desire to bother one person. I certainly didn't want the cop to circle back around to find me still standing here. This was only going to work if I was *smooth*.

"You know," I start, then pause. I've gotten more recruits today than I usually do in three weeks. I call the day a success. "I'm getting ready for a break. We can go home."

"Sounds good to me." Dad's lips curl into his proud dad smile, and we fall into step together and head toward his car.

"Afterall, I can come back tomorrow."

NINE
Christian

My phone's on silent mode. I don't want to deal with any calls right now, but I catch it lighting up. It's Arielle, my little sister, who is attending her first semester of college, and hasn't exactly been attending classes. My gaze wafts through the Coffee Loft, not a soul in sight. I unlocked the door, but I need to check my doorstep. I don't doubt something is *up*, but I can wait a minute and welcome the distraction. "Hey, El."

There's hesitation on the other line before I hear a quiet and out of character, "Heeeey."

My brows pinch together as I adjust the phone to hear better. "What's wrong?"

"Can I come stay with you for a while?"

"Here?" I straighten my spine, my attention lasering in on this conversation. "You mean, in New York?"

"Yeah, I can sleep on the floor. It's not a big deal."

"Wait a second." I pace forward, sorting out previous conversations we'd had. Nothing we'd spoken about sounded as if she was in trouble. Still, my big-brother alarm sounds. "What's going on? Why would you leave college in the middle of the year?"

"Let's say college isn't my thing."

"El," I press her name firmly. "You know I'll do anything to help you. Be honest. Why are you quitting school?"

"I didn't quit." A crackle of air blows into her phone, projecting loudly on my end. "I sort of lost interest. Now, there isn't a point."

"El," I say softer this time, echoing her sobriety. "I won't judge you, but are you sure you want to quit this close to the end? You never know. Sometimes it looks worse than it is. You already have half of the year done. It's worth it to wait." I swallow, waiting for her to fill in the conversation with her usual chatter, but nothing comes. "El?"

My sister is a talker, and the only reason she'd ever be quiet in a serious conversation is if she's fighting back tears. I'm more practical than her. I would be stubborn and finish school, but I understood her nature. If she had already quit with her heart, there was no point in her body staying there.

"Ah, sure. You can stay. I'm in a tiny hotel room, but I'll call the desk to change to a two-bed." I want to ask her if she has an idea of how long she was staying. However, the lack of her usual chattiness tells me she isn't in the mood to talk. "When should I expect you?"

"Like ten minutes."

I check my watch, even though I don't need it to compute that math. She could not drive or even fly from Massachusetts that fast. "Are you teleporting?"

"Nah, I got an early start." She pauses for a beat. This is the part where I would normally tease her, but her tonal inflections warn me not to. I wait for her to offer further explanation. Even after the longest silence—one that was so stale, it made me cringe—the only thing she whispers is, "Thanks, Christian."

"Yeah, you bet," I mumble into the phone. Not because I wasn't sincere, but I am doing my best to hide my concern. "See ya soon."

The conversation falls into silence, and I set my phone down. The tension in the back of my head immediately swells. I'm unable to support myself. I've dug a deep hole with this Coffee Loft, and there is no way I can help her, too.

But *not* helping her is not an option either.

I rub my temples, wishing for a pressure valve I can crank to release the strain in my head. It does nothing but make me feel overwhelmed. I force a positive thought. "Well, if anything, Arielle can work the counter while I get a job that actually makes money." I laugh, not in a funny way. My fingers jitter with anxiety, like they want to play a piano. I've never played in my life. That's new. Maybe not the best sign.

Perhaps a coffee can help?

I walk behind the counter, ready my shot glasses for espresso, deciding to switch to half-caff, hoping the reduced caffeine will be better for sudden new jitters. There's no way I can switch to decaf cold turkey. My counter is perfectly shining, and my grinders are packed to the top with beans the way I left them yesterday when I closed. Nothing is out of place, even though the store's been open for almost an hour. I hate how clean it is. I haven't had one customer. I checked both sides of the block when I switched the sign from closed to open, and Portia wasn't there *yet*. I assume it's only a matter of time.

I'm at a loss for what to do with her if she comes back. What are my options? Maybe file a restraining order for harassment? I can't sit back and let her ruin my business.

A cold breeze wafts through the air, drawing my attention to the open front door.

Immediate surge of adrenaline.

Not a customer.

"Boy, you must have been sitting in the parking lot." I smile genuinely as Arielle stomps between the narrow pass of tables. A knit beanie sits on her head, with her not-showered blonde hair hanging out at the bottom. She's wearing that scowl she became famous for. The one that says, I'm-not-a-morning person. Now that I see she's safe in one piece, I can't resist teasing her. "Who stole your puppy?"

She plants her feet on the other side of the counter, glaring as if she whole-heartedly believes I stole her make-believe puppy. She has so much disdain clouding her ordinarily bright blue eyes, I'm thinking I need to check the backroom for a dog. "What did I do?" I seal my coffee cup lid and take a sip. "Are you going to tell me what's going on, or do I call Dad and tell him that you're here—"

"No." Her hand flies up in a stop motion. "Don't call Dad. Not before I get a job, or he'll make me come home to work for him."

"Then you better start talking." Completely understanding her dread of not wanting to work for a construction company, I motion to the table behind her. I pull out a chair for her, taking the one across from it for myself. "Are you in trouble?"

She sinks into the chair, dropping a sigh that borders on a whimper. "No trouble. Just sick." Before I have time to scan her for symptoms, she plants her gaze right on mine. "Heartsick."

My shoulders drop as everything makes sense. Of course, this is about a man. That's why she's here. She expects me to enlighten her about my species. As every time before, I have nothing to do but shrug. "Who do you need me to beat up?"

A tiny curve tips upward on her lips as she knows I talk a big talk with my big ego, but I couldn't punch a fly. "Trust me, I wish that was an option."

I wave my hand out, putting my empty lobby on display. "I got nothing going on here. Might as well take it out on some sorry loser."

"He's not a loser." Her quick defense reveals more than she planned, and she bites her bottom lip, as if trying to take it back.

I take a sip of coffee, and then stare out over the empty chairs and tables. Something about having Arielle sitting here with me makes sense. Maybe that's what I need? A partner. She sure looks like she could use a friend right now. We always made a good sibling team, getting into trouble, or rather out-of-trouble together.

I am in trouble this time. If anyone can help me get out of trouble, it will be her. "Well, I'll let you stay on one condition." I point a disciplinary finger at her. "You have one week to tell Dad. I don't want this coming back at me."

Her jaw drops as I wave my finger at her, and she doesn't even stutter out a broken rebuttal. "Yeah, that's fine. Whatever." As if trying to force a change of subject, her gaze dances around the room. "Why is no one here?"

Now it's my turn to glare, as I push back my chair, ready to investigate on my own. "I'm wondering the same thing. Let's go see why."

Ten

Portia

Unable to stop humming, I steer Mrs. Nelson's dog back to the apartment building from our morning recruiting walk. My app is exploding with new users. After yesterday's promotion, the word finally got out, and I'm getting organic signups. *Paying ones!*

I'm late to the coffee shop, but not fretting because my app is literally running itself. Every time I log in, there are new users and I have no idea where they came from. Finally, being one step ahead of the process is a much-needed stress relief.

I let out a sigh as we climb the stairs. Me, two steps at a time. Oliver, four steps at a time, as he has massive bandwidth. His nails scratch the cement, and his dog tags jingle as we round the final corner to his home. I knock on his door, calling out. "We're back."

Mrs. Nelson is hard of hearing. She doesn't admit it, but I suspect she's also hard of seeing. The evidence being, it doesn't matter what time of day I show up, she always has one random sponge curler in her hair which she seemingly overlooked. I pound on the door because it's the only way she hears me. "Mrs. Nelson, Oliver's home!"

Pressing my ear to the door, I hear nothing. Not even the pop of her recliner chair folding back up. "Mrs. Nelson!" I rise to the tips of my toes, nearly smashing my nose against the pane while I peer through the lace curtains on the tiny top door window. Everything is dark. She's not home. One would think it odd, but I don't even shrug. She's awfully forgetful. It's not the first time, or even the second or third, she has forgotten I have Oliver, and she leaves to run an errand.

Usually, I don't mind because I could certainly take him for another lap to top off my recruits. Today, I'm anxious to get to the coffee shop. "We're here!" I holler at the top of my lungs and twist the doorknob, hoping it will budge enough for me to slip Oliver inside. The knob is as tight as my dad's pickle jar lids.

Speaking of Dad, I sure wish he were here. He'd take Oliver until Mrs. Nelson returns, but my parents have a weekend wedding out of town. They left this morning. I check the time on my phone. It's well past Coffee Loft opening time. If I don't get there for the morning rush, there will be no point. My website is busy today, but how long will it last? I surely can't get cocky because I have one good day. I need to keep recruiting.

I tap my foot, weighing my options. Before I talk myself out of it, I spin on my heel and head down the stairs. Oliver's going to hang out with me today. He's probably ready for a nap. He'll be fine.

I giggle as I pull my lips into a dubious grin.

Christian will *love* him.

I'm whistling by the time I steer Oliver to Coffee Loft. There is a small line of people lingering on the Coffee Loft sidewalk. Not in front of the door waiting to get in. Most of them appear to be waiting to go down the subway entrance. I sidestep, avoiding getting in their way, and giggle, visualizing Christian's glowing scarlet face peering out the window to see me.

I'm not a mean person. I've never met a person I didn't like. Well, until Christian. It's not to say I hate him, more I hate what he did. I'm not afraid to stand up for what was right. It isn't right for Christian to fire both Jade and me on

Christmas Eve. Especially after we ran that store for weeks by ourselves without even a day off.

Plus, this is the best location for female recruits because of all the high-end fashion boutiques in the area. Unless I want to go into New York City, this is the perfect place for me. Also, it's a teeny bit fun to taunt him with my presence. I slowly pass in front of the glass door but resist the urge to press my face to the glass and wave like a crazy person. Instead, I paste on my stoic expression and raise my chin.

"Good morning!" I call out to everyone. "Would anybody like a free match on my dating website? It's called, Your Last First Date, and I have a 100% match success rate."

I snap for Oliver to sit next to me, and he's obedient enough. Mostly because he's tired, and he lays down with his giant tongue almost grazing the ground. "Are you ready for the weekend?" I ask Mr. Donold. He's a retired accountant who lives alone, but steps out every morning for a fresh bagel from the grocery store. I have no idea how long he's been single, but he dresses fairly nicely with tan trousers, and a button shirt every day. He could certainly attract a woman. No matter how often I insist he try my app, he refuses. For some reason, he hasn't told me to bug off about it yet. With an encouraging smile, I tack on, "I can get you matched for a date today."

He tsks, but I'm not offended. This is what he does. It's a game we have. "Someday," I go on, "I'll get you signed up." Now that I've caught my breath from rushing over here, I glance down at Oliver, who suddenly stands in alert, doing his signature I-found-hunk-excited-tail wag.

"What do you see, boy?" I raise my gaze, but it is too late. I don't have a tight grip on his leash, and he takes off. His force is too strong for my unprepared hands. I grapple at the end of the leash, but my hands are full, and everything jumbles together. It's useless. All my cards scatter to the ground, and Oliver is *gone*.

Eleven

Christian

Out of nowhere, a massive beast of an animal swoops in from behind me and jumps on my chest, knocking me off balance. I stumble back, flailing my arms. He's so massive, he blocks my view. I take one too many steps back, and my heel teases the edge of a subway staircase. I windmill my arms backward, fighting the urge to fall, but it's no use. I tumble, taking the beast with me. I wail out in pain as my back twists in an unnatural way, and my head pounds against each concrete stair ledge over and over. One, two, three steps, and I finally stop rolling, but I drop down a fourth step from the sheer weight of this creature on top of me.

This is undoubtedly a premeditated attack.

Someone is trying to kill me.

As I plop down yet another stair, my cheek is met with a warm, velvety tongue and slobber. Cringing, I open my eyes. "Stop!" I wail out, and stretch my neck, trying to free my face from his washing, but the beast must think we're playing. "Get off me!" I yell, finding my lungs again. "I can barely breathe." Surprise. He doesn't listen. I find my bearings enough to shove him off me as I totter to a standing position. Dizzy, and not at all feeling the way standing should, I've developed a bit of a hunch from the spasms in my lower back that won't stop rocketing all the way down through my leg. I brace one palm on my back while grasping the stair rail with my free hand and hiss, "Go home, doggie."

He sits his massive furry bottom on the top stairs, taking watch over me, not moving. I don't waste time talking to him again, but there's a niggling in my brain wondering where he came from. Something could have happened to his owner. A shrill voice meets my ear, "Not that man, Oliver!" Portia's standing at the top of the stairwell, her jaw hanging low.

"I'm so sorry." She hobbles down the top two stairs, grabbing the beast by the collar with one hand and securing the end of the leash in her other. "He's trained to run after hunks—I mean, *men*. I had no idea you were even here." Her gaze skirts to the side. "Are you okay?"

Straightening my back as much as I can with my new hunch, I mutter, "Yeah. I'm totally fine."

She opens her mouth to speak. Nothing comes out. Then she tries again. "You don't look well?" Her cadence sounds more like a question.

I pivot, wincing as my back spasms, and I suck in a loud gasp.

"Wait a second." Stepping forward, her brows lower. "You're hurt."

"I'm f-fine," I squeak, my voice a tad high. Clearing my throat, I try again as I readjust my hand position lower on my back. "Just a little back pain. Nothing a little rest won't solve." The world is spinning, as I clearly hit my head harder than I thought. I slide my foot up a step, gluing a plastic smirk on my face. All the while, I'm crying for my momma in heaven on the inside, with pain imploding in my back.

"Are you sure?" She moves down another step closer, the dog still on the leash, but he's sitting quite well for her. I turn my face, desperate to hide the beads of sweat I can feel forming on my forehead. "Did you break something?"

"Nope. Everything's good as new." I slide another foot up, faster this time to prove my point. "Nothing I can't shake off. Bye now. Have a nice life." With a death grip on the rail, I suck in air, and snake my foot up another step, all the while trying not to howl out in agony. There's no way I can let her—of all people— see me cry. I wobble as the world continues to spiral around my head.

"I don't mean to pry, but you look broken." This time her hand meets my shoulder, and a lightning bolt splices through my arm. If I hadn't been malfunctioning before, this completes the job. I immobilize, resigning myself to the fact that I'll be stuck on this stair forever. "You took a good tumble down these stairs. Maybe you should get checked out by someone?"

Her hand moves down my arm, meeting my hand that's braced on my back. Even though her hand is tender and warm, her touch pricks my skin, sending tingles back through my arm. "I'm f-fine." I shake off her hand. "It's not like you're a nurse."

"No, I'm not a nurse, but I can tell when someone is injured. You are hunched over, and you never used to stand like that."

I slip a toe on the top stair and straighten my back as much as I can, but my back spasms from the tiniest movement. I push through it. I need to get out of here before I do—or say—something stupid. I certainly don't need her touching me again.

"You look unstable. You need to lie down. Let me help you back to the store—"

"You can't come back to my store!" I blurt out. El will be curious about Portia and concerned about me. She doesn't need to be either. That can never happen. There's no way I can ever let Portia into my store again. There's a reason I had to let her go because she's—

My mind goes blank. Portia's hand is on my arm again as she takes the rest of the steps, closing the gap between us. "You have the most soured expression on your face. You're either in massive pain, or something else is bothering you. What's wrong?"

"Nothing's bothering me." I shake my head, but that throws off the last little balance I have, and I'm back in orbit, spinning around. So dizzy.

Run! But I can't run. I can't even hobble, but I desperately want to leave, and she won't leave me alone.

"Wait a second." Her head does that tilting thing it does when she's thinking. I don't like it. "You don't look well."

"Nope. Sure don't." I inhale deeply, my stomach dropping a full inch as the stairwell continues orbiting. "Uh." I need to sit down. Everything is whirling around my head. I grip the rail harder, focusing on my inhalations. Even though I'm sure she's holding her hand steady, my vision is so off kilter, her hand appears to wave in front of me like a white flag.

I need a white flag.

I also need to get out of here. "Whatever," I mutter as I fumble forward. I must get out of here before I pass out from pain. I take more steps.

I kept waiting for the world to go dark, but somehow I pace the twelve steps back to my store safely-one painful step at a time.

Then everything goes dark.

TWELVE

Portia

"Don't you have someone you can call?" I stand over Christian as he lays flat on the sidewalk after collapsing. Oliver sits next to me, arching his gaze up. I can smell his expectation for me to congratulate him on catching a "hunk." I bite my cheek. Christian is *not* a hunk.

Christian's not doing well.

His karma from firing me brought real pain.

Or maybe it's not karma. I stare at Christian wincing in pain. *I* failed to control Oliver. Maybe it's a very expensive lawsuit if he decides to be litigious?

I'm not happy about this one bit. Even if it's the single person who fired me on Christmas, I must help him because the accident is Oliver's fault. Since Oliver is my responsibility—*it's my fault.*

"I'm fine." He mumbles over the double chin he creates when he winces. He rolls on to his side while bracing his lower back with one hand.

The Coffee Loft door flies open, and out comes a literal model. Blonde hair wafting down her back, and alabaster skin so flawless it was smoother than French silk. "What happened?" her words burst with importance.

"Ah, he fell down some stairs and tried to walk. He might have a concussion."

"I'm fine," Christian's high-pitched demand bellows from below us. It gets even worse when he tries to pull himself to a seated position. His death rattle rolls out, causing me to gasp in shock.

"Let me help you." The model swoops in, bracing up Christian as he stumbles to his feet. I cower with my eyes wide as they waddle together back to the building.

He's seriously injured, and Oliver did that.

Fear swooshes through my body.

I don't want to get Oliver in trouble. Or worse, Mrs. Nelson. I'm the one who taught Oliver to run after hunks—*men*. The recruiting game is an innocent thing we do. Oliver wasn't supposed to hurt anyone. *This is my fault*! "Can I help?" I stammer, stepping forward to open the door. Before my palm brushes against the handle, Christian hollers loudly, jolting my nerves.

I jerk my thumb over my shoulder, taking an alarmed step back. "Maybe I should just go?"

"Stop screaming." The woman wraps her arm all the way around him. "You sound like you are dying."

"I'm not dying." Christian's weakened voice wafts out. "It's just my back. I sprained it."

I'm screaming in my head while my feet plant on the floor. *Don't go inside! It's a trap. Since when do I help people who fire me?*

The woman speaks so gently, as if she's taking care of an infant. "Let's get you to your office to lay down on the couch."

My stomach wrenches, and I combat the urge to grab it as I try to remain tough. There are a lot of things in life I detest, but high on my list of "things I can't stomach" are people in pain. Against all my better judgment, I cower in the doorway, vowing to not let even a toe inside ever again.

It is a betrayal to step inside this place!

Christian's huffing out heaving breaths each time he exhales.

The woman's perfect-mother-hen voice rolls out. "Maybe you broke something?"

"It's not the pain that's bothering me." Christian's lips purse into a perfect O while he blows out an even breath. "I've blown out my back before. It takes days to be able to walk. I can't work on my feet. Eventually I'll be fine, but my store will be bankrupt by then."

My gaze skirts the empty Coffee Loft lobby. Life's been more than a little crazy lately. There isn't much I am sure of, but something jiggles inside of me. I need to protect Oliver and Mrs. Nelson. "Don't worry about getting back to work," I rush, persuasively. "I can help out."

"Thanks, but no thanks." His sarcastic tone cackles out.

The woman nods toward me. "Do you know her?"

"Ah, she used to work here," he mumbles over his double chin again.

"Oh, that's perfect." Her posture springs up like a zipper cinching along the spine. "She knows what to do, and she can help out while you rest."

"No. Nope. Not perfect—"

"I'm Arielle." Her excitement bubbles out with her gaze locking on me, all the while she speaks over Christian, "I'm Christian's sister. We'd love it if you will help us." Now she's stroking Christian's back as if he's a long-haired cat. It helps to keep his sarcasm at bay as they continue to the office at a snail's pace.

I finger tap my chin, hating this whole thing. What choice did I have? I caused this mess. I need to fix it. A scuffle at my feet reminds me I'm still trailing Oliver. He's pulling on the leash, like a moth fighting for freedom from its own spun cocoon. "Let me run home first, and drop him off, and I'll be back."

"That would be wonderful," Arielle calls back.

Or maybe I won't come back! My eyes are about to bug out of my head.

Why do I have all the bad luck?

"Yeah." I run a hand through my hair, tucking it behind my ear. "I mean, I can help for an hour or two while he rests. Maybe for the rest of the day—"

"Perfect." Arielle leans over, practically heaving Christian further through his office door. "That would be amazing. Thank you so much!"

I can't hear anything else. My ears are bleeding, and I walk forward until my feet meet the doorframe. Slamming my forehead against the muted-eggshell paint, I suppress a scream.

Is this happening?

Is my luck really getting even worse?

First, I was fired. Then the dog I borrowed to run my business—so I don't go homeless—broke the jerk who fired me. I just offered to *help* him!

I throw up my hands as my shoulders bounce, preluding to sobs I'm holding in with all my strength. I've got to hurry and get Oliver home. Maybe if I can cover Christian's customers, he won't threaten to sue me or Mrs. Nelson?

This is the worst possible thing that could have happened today!

THIRTEEN
Christian

"Why did you do that?" I whisper harshly to my sister. "That woman is my nemesis, and you invited her into my space."

Arielle always has an uncanny ability to be best friends with everyone. She's a Labrador of people. I knew better than to let her talk to Portia, but it's not like I had a choice. Portia was spying on me. Now I'm stuck. Literally, and figuratively. I sprawl out on the couch in my office, and I can't even wiggle my big toe.

If I tell Portia she can't help, I'll look like a total jerk. Plus, I know from the last time I threw out my back, I'm going to be off my feet for at least a day or two. Arielle isn't trained to run the store. But Portia could train her. Maybe

if Portia can show her the ropes this afternoon, I won't
need any more help from her?

"Christian, relax." Arielle peeps back into my office
door from the lobby. "Nobody's here yet. You're not losing any business."

"That's not helping the matter," I grumble.

"But look what I found lying on the ground outside."
El flashes a postcard in front me. "It's a QR code for a free
match on this new dating website called, *Your Last First
Date*. You should sign up. It would give you something to
do while you're lying there, and it might help that mood
thing you've been having."

I flash a look at the ceiling. There's nothing wrong with
my mood. I'm not signing up for a stupid dating site.
"That's the dumbest thing I've ever heard."

"Come on." Without waiting for an invite, she takes a
giant step inside the door, crossing the room to snatch my
phone off my desk. Then she plops to the floor, sitting next
to me. "There's nobody here, and it will kill time. It might
be fun."

"Not doing that—" Shuffling my feet from annoyance,
I wince when it pulls my back muscle.

"Great!" El cuts me off while pulling up a bright pink
website on my phone. It's the most disgusting thing I've
seen all day, but it doesn't even phase her as she types. "I've
been worried about you. This is the perfect thing to take
your mind off all the stress you have here."

"That's the last thing I need."

"Look at how cute the website is," El gushes, ignoring my defenses. "And look." She points to the screen, her lips twisting into a giddy grin. "You can pick your preferences!" She adjusts the angle of my phone, her whole face lighting up from the glow of the screen. "Let's see...what do you like? Kindhearted. Professional. Family oriented, and we'll add good looks for fun."

El's clicking buttons I can't see from my spot of slamming the back of my head against the armrest. I don't doubt she is making me look like a giant tool on there. Again, Arielle's always been social with everyone. This is right up her alley. "You should be the one making the profile."

"Oh, no, I'm not on the market at the moment, but you totally are."

I can't stand to be here, wasting my time with this, but I can't move, so I'm out of options.

"Look!" El peels her eyes from the screen, sliding it so I can see it. "You got a match!"

"I did?" I hesitate, straining my gaze to see what she looks like but there's no photo. "Where's she at?"

"You don't get a photo until you unlock that feature after a successful chat. Let me send her a message for you!" El beams at me before her fingers glide back over the keyboard. "This is going to be so perfect."

Not perfect. It's the definition of insanity that I would let my sister do this. I don't need to chat with anyone. I don't need a date app. All I need is my back to feel better so I can get off this floor and run my business!

Fourteen

Portia

I dab the tear in the corner of my eye while squinting at the scathing review one man left on my website. I had stopped inside my apartment after dropping Oliver off, and couldn't resist logging into the back office of my site for a quick check. Now I wish I hadn't.

Reviewer - Waste of time. Don't bother. I signed up and kept getting error messages before it even gave me a match. It's a scam.

A line of perspiration beads on my lower back. With all the organic traffic on my app yesterday, I had an influx of men. The men were matching, taking the woman out of the match portal. There are *no women left*. Men are getting error messages. This has never happened before.

I've always had enough people to at least give them one match to keep them busy chatting.

What am I going to do? I don't have time to find more women. I promised Christian I'd come back to the store to help him. If Dad were here, I could send him out. He doesn't come home until tomorrow. By then I could have more bad reviews!

A horrible thought creeps into my brain.

I can make a fake profile and chat with these men until I get more women.

Should I?

I inhale deeply, weighing that option. It's not the right option. It could backfire in the worst way. But then again, how would anyone find out? A lump rises in my throat, but I swallow it down. I'm not scamming people. That's not what my company stands for. I would rather the app goes on hiatus for a few weeks than do that.

But if it went on hiatus, I might not be able to redeem it. I might get so many bad reviews it would never recover. Not to mention, this is my time to fly this ship. Yeah, I know ships don't fly. Sail it. Whatever. I need this app. I sank all my savings into it. It's my one shot at becoming financially independent and finding freedom from my drudgery at the coffee shop.

Sure, Dad could give me money until I find something else. I don't want to do that anymore. I'm nearly thirty.

There's something about being thirty and needing to ask your dad for rent money that feels dehumanizing.

My app flashes another error message. Someone tried to match, and it didn't work. It is Thursday, one of our busier days, as people match for the weekend. I stare at my wall, feeling as if the room is shrinking, closing in on me. This is bad. I must figure something out.

Without thinking twice—I don't have time for guilt—I go to the new client scene, racing to create a profile. Yep, my mind is made up. I must save all my hard work.

I don't need to lie, because it doesn't ask for my name or photo. I quickly select preferences from the drop-down menus of what I'm looking for.

Male.

Career oriented.

Family values.

Good looks.

Kind-hearted.

That got me into the portal, where there are a series of more detailed questions to narrow down the search. I don't narrow it down. I want to match with as many men as possible to keep them on my app until I can get real women.

Sweat pools in the center of my palms by the time I click the Match Me button. A heart thumps on the screen while it finds my matches, and I let out a heavy breath.

I can't believe I'm doing this.

But what choice do I have?

Just this once, because Dad's out of town, and I don't have any time to get ahead. If this doesn't qualify as an emergency, then I don't know what does.

The screen switches to one that looks like a Guess Who board, filling each square with a match. Twelve! I matched with twelve. That's good. Not enough. There's still going to be some men who won't get matches.

Why did this have to happen now?

My computer chimed with a message!

Already?

Boy, that was fast. Now I must message back.

What am I going to say?

Forget what!

I need to leave before Christian gets even madder at me.

Oops, another chime.

And another.

My adrenaline surges all the way to my neck. I can't chat with all these men! What did I just do? I opened a tsunami of ethical issues.

A knot in my throat swells, making it hard for me to breathe. If I tell all these men I'm too busy to chat, they will want another match at some point. All this did was buy me a little time. Not much time. This can't be happening!

The lump in my throat pulsates, but this time when I try to swallow it down, it lodges tight, not budging.

Everything I have worked for this last year and all the savings I dumped into this app flash through my mind. If I don't get the ratio balanced soon, I'll be inundated with bad reviews. Reviews that stay online *forever*. My app is too new to absorb all those bad reviews. I'll be buried by them.

I want so badly to yank my hair because I'm frustrated. Instead, I scream out, overwhelmed as tears flood my eyes.

Don't panic. I breathe into a new thought. I must stay positive.

I didn't make it this far to fail now.

I quickly swap my status to say I'm interested in chatting but busy. Then I race to the coffee shop, vowing to respond to all of the messages in between customers.

Christian

With my gaze pinned to the floor—thanks to this lovely new back hunch—I hobble out of my office into the lobby and brace a hand on the wall. "What did I miss?"

One of Arielle's penciled on brows rises above the other. "Absolutely nothing. This place is a dive."

"Thanks, sis."

"I watched a ton of YouTube videos teaching me how to make these coffees. Oh!" She flashes a jug at me. "Which reminds me, you're down to your last almond milk."

"So, let me get this straight. Not only are you not making any money, but you are using all my resources. Perfect."

"Well, I have to practice somehow. I had two lattes already, and I'm buzzed. I think you should try one of these almond milk lattes." She points to the nutrition label on the side of the jug. "Look at how much less sugar it has. It's a lot better for your insulin levels. It may help stabilize your mood."

"Nothing's wrong with my mood, or my insulin." I scoff. If I could walk, I would run over there, grab that jug and chuck it to prove my point. I don't need anything special to help my mood. I'm not moody. She's moody. Why is she even talking about moods? "Are you a doctor now?"

Arielle backed up against the counter, lifting herself to sit directly on it, with her feet hanging down. I glare at her. "Nobody wants your butt on the place you put their drink."

She cringes, muttering, "Almond milk will fix your mood," as she slides off the counter. "How is your back?" My heart tanks to a whole new low as I toss a discreet glare out the front door, watching the people walk *past* without even looking inside. "Fine."

"You're not fine." Arielle tilted her head, giving me an angled stare.

"How would you know?" I button my bottom lip, not wanting to leak even the slightest clue that my back is erupting in pain at this very moment.

"I can tell because your brows are beaded together. That lady should be back any minute to help." She checks her watch. "Then you can rest. What did you say her name is?"

I scowl at El. It's absurd she's even suggesting I receive help from someone who was literally running off my customers only moments earlier. Nobody on the planet has that level of patience. "Her name's Portia, and I fired her. She steals all my Oreos and was sabotaging me."

"I hope she doesn't sue you."

My eyes slide side to side as I mull her comment. "What do you mean?"

Arielle readies the espresso machine by wiping off the steamer with a damp rag. "Her dog had an accident on *your* property—"

"Public property," I cut in. "The cop even confirmed the sidewalk is public property, and I have no right to kick her off. Nobody can claim the subway."

"Hmm." She presses the espresso button for shots and pours milk into the steaming cup. "I almost wonder, though, if she couldn't fight that. You know, it's like how you must shovel snow from the sidewalk of your business, but you don't own it. You can get sued if someone slips. Did you notice if the dog was hurt?"

"Nah. It's not icy. It's nothing I did." I shake my head vehemently. "There's no way she can blame this on me. She was trespassing." My thoughts recoil in my head, while Arielle noisily steams the milk. Somewhere in the last hour she taught herself to run that machine fairly well, and I sit back, observing. Maybe Arielle coming to visit wasn't such a bad idea? She can help me work until I can get back on my feet.

Arielle divides the milk into two cups, adds the shots, and seals the cups with their lids. "For your mood." She hands me a cup, tacking on, "Just try it."

I'm famished, craving something to take the edge off my tumultuous morning. One little sip won't hurt. I press my lips to the lid, doing a temperature check. Who knows if Arielle actually knows what she is doing? However, the temp is perfect, and I lift the cup until the first taste meets my tongue, and it is a little liquid heaven. Delicious. So smooth, with a little nutty undertone, giving it a hearty flavor. "That's good."

"Told ya." She takes a long sip of hers before lowering her cup and trapping my eyes in a lock.

"What now?" I eye her cup, remembering how two minutes ago she said she'd had enough coffee, and now she is downing a third latte. She is expensive to keep around.

"She's pretty. I wonder if she's single?"

"No!" I bleep out, but then play dumb. "Who are you even talking about? Who's pretty? Maybe you should go get me some more almond milk since you're drinking all mine, and the delivery truck doesn't come until next week."

She watches me coyly over the lid of her cup while taking a long sip. "I don't have my license."

"What license? You don't need a license to buy almond milk."

"Driver's license. I'll have to take a bus or something. It would be way complicated, especially since I have no idea how this city's laid out."

"There's a grocery store next door. Wait a second . . ." I set my cup down. "How'd you drive here without your license?"

"I never said I drove. You said I drove. I took a cab from the airport."

"Okay. How you'd lose your license?" I study her face. She never lies to me. Not that she hasn't tried, but I can tell because her left eye twitches. It isn't moving now. It's beaming forward, completely unwavering.

"It's kind of dumb, but I had a bunch of parking tickets from parking on the street at school. They were out of parking permits by the time I went to buy one. There wasn't anywhere to park unless I wanted to walk a mile. Apparently, when you don't pay your tickets, you get a court date. I didn't know I had a court date because my car registration went to Dad's address. Since I never call home, he didn't bother to let me know. Since I didn't know, I didn't show."

"You're kidding." Scratching the back of my head, I wonder if I missed some family drama. Neither El, nor I had ever avoided Dad. "Why haven't you called home?"

"No, big reason. I wasn't ready to tell Dad about school, and I knew I could never lie to him."

"He more than likely has figured it out, but he is probably giving you space until you come to him. You know he's not confrontational."

"Right." Her gaze pulls to the floor. "I didn't want to stress him out while I try to figure out my life."

"El, what's going on with you?" Momentarily forgetting that I'm the hunchback of Notre Dame incarnate, I step forward, but immediately halt while I emit a loud hiss and grab my lower back. *Not doing that again.* I'm still concerned about El. "This isn't like you."

"I know." She inhales deeply before pulling her lips to force a lopsided grin. "I lost myself at school, but I'm trying hard to get out of this funk. I need to get away from that town for a while. You know, since it's my hometown. I think I could heal here."

The pressure valve on my headache cranked up to double speed. I'm drowning in this Coffee Loft. I can do that because I only have myself to take care of. I did that on purpose because I have goals. That sounds selfish, but I don't want anyone else to sacrifice the way I'm forcing myself to do. I want so badly to tell Arielle not to worry. She can stay here if she needs to. With zero sales, I don't know how long *I* can stay here.

I can't tell her that.

"It's going to be okay." I pull my lips into a complicit grin. "You can stay here if you need to."

Sixteen
Portia

"That's awful, Mom." I take long strides back to the coffee shop with my phone glued to my ear, and I glare at the overcast sky. This winter has been brutal as it dumps snow every day. I hoped to hear my parents had made it home. "I'm sorry the airline is jerking you around like that. You're right to rent a car to drive."

"Yeah, it'll be a long haul, but we're tired of waiting." Mom's surprisingly optimistic tone rings through the phone. "If everything goes well, we should be in late tonight. Is everything still okay there?"

"Yep," I quip as fast as I can. "Everything's . . . excellent."

"Good. Did you and Oliver catch anything this morning?"

Christian flashes in my mind, causing my breath to hitch in my chest. I'm not sure why I'm uneasy. It's something Oliver and I do all the time. What will my parents think when they learn I hurt someone? "Ah, just one guy, but he isn't interested in the site."

"Really?" Mom audibly scoffs. "That's too bad. Well, when we get back, Dad will take you to Home Hardware. That always works."

"Yeah, it sure does." I hover my finger over the End Call button. Leaving out the major details about what I'm really doing brings a wave of nausea to my gut. "Gotta go."

"Love you," Mom sings into the phone.

"Love you, too." I end the call, feeling hopeful about my afternoon at the Coffee Loft. Hopefully Christian is resting, and not monitoring me, because I need to reply to these messages.

The Coffee Loft hardly looks open as I pass through the empty cafe, each table neatly put together without so much as a coffee ring stain. The lights are on, and the soft music station hums in the background, but there is no sign of customers anywhere. I adjust my French press while straining my neck to see behind the counter into the office. "Boy, I really did steal all of your customers," I jokingly call out, still pacing forward before I have eyes on Christian.

A cacophony of crashing sounds explodes from behind the counter, and a few random plastic drink cups roll, followed by Christian's front hair spike slowly peeking over the ledge. His already round eyes swell larger when he sees me. "What is that thing you are holding?"

I halt. Maybe this is a bad idea? "Uh, pardon my French press." I set it down on the table nearest me. "It's my favorite way to make coffee, and if I'm going to work all day, I need a fresh cup."

Christian's narrow face grows even longer as his jaw drops. "I told you Coffee Loft doesn't make French press—"

"Portia!" Arielle flies out of the backroom, swooping into our conversation, cutting off Christian. She's already standing next to me with an uplifted brow of concern pinned on her face. "We're so glad to have you back." She waves me back behind the counter. "Grab an apron, and I'll make you a drink on the house. We just unpacked the Coffee Loft special blend. You have to try it. It will make you toss your French press for good."

Christian's mouth flaps open. "You—"

Arielle gives him a stony glare and speaks over him. "Christian's been telling me how awful he feels about letting you go. It's been a big misunderstanding. He's truly ecstatic for the second chance." She breezes behind the counter. As she walks past Christian, she places her hand on his jaw, physically closing his gaping mouth. He doesn't crack a smile, but I stifle a giggle.

"What would you like to drink?" She positions herself behind the bar, hand hovering over the stacks of cups, waiting for my instructions.

"Ah, it's fine. I can use my French press."

Christian's head jerks back, as he immediately goes off balance, lifting his foot. My guess is Arielle stomped on it because his voice squawks as he grumbles, "No, I insist. You're helping. It's the least I could do to *pay* for your drinks."

Giving up, I guess I could try their *special* blend. "Let's do a skinny, cinnamon dulce, half-caff since it's afternoon already."

"Absolutely." She snatches the large cup—the one we call Lofty—and sets it on the counter. "That's Christian's favorite flavor. You two have so much in common. I can already tell you'll get along fine now that everything is behind you."

Christian robotically pivots, hunching over as if gravity is too strong for him to fight. He silently hobbles to his office, and pulls the door closed behind him. Another cacophony of noise rumbles out from behind his closed door. Arielle pauses, locking her eyes on me, and giggles. "He takes some warming up, but I promise he'll be fine once you get past this stage. What kind of schedule do you like?"

I meander up to the bar, waiting for my coffee. "How about a shift when Christian isn't here?"

"If you want to open tomorrow, that would be great. I was going to do it, but I would love to sleep in. I hate morning shifts." She presses the lid on my cup and hands it to me over the bar.

"Thank you." I receive the drink. "That's perfect."

"Christian changed the code for the keypad, but I'll text you the new one." She waves her hand over the coffee brewing station. "Everything else should be the same."

"Sounds good."

"Alright, if you are okay here then, I might slip out and run to the drug store to get Christian some pain meds." She flashes her hand up. "Unless you need anything?"

I can't believe I'm about to work for Christian, but I don't want him to retaliate against Oliver. "I should be fine."

"Sounds good." She spins on her heel, heading toward the door. "I'll see you in a jiffy."

"Absolutely." I wave my hand, knowing fully well Christian's head will explode if he sees me running this place alone. I stare at his closed office door. It's clear he's staying locked in there as long as I'm here. My gaze paces the lobby, and there's no one here.

That's probably my fault since most of my customers confessed to staying away since I was fired.

I smash my lips into a thinking cinch while pulling out my phone to stare at my app.

Might as well chat with these guys.

I have about a dozen choices. Since I'm only at level one, I can't see any photos or even their names. Nobody sticks out over the others. That's one of the features I built into the app. Scrolling for something to stand out, a message pops up from one of them, and I tap on it.

Heyyyyyy Profile 421! How are you? Fun fact. The more Ys people have in their greeting, the more interesting they are.

I snicker at the cheesy joke that reminds me of my dad's jokes and reply.

He

I press send and drum my fingers along the counter, waiting to see if this dude has a sense of humor.

After several minutes of no reply, Arielle breezes back through the door with a grocery sack. "See, I told you I would be fast."

I stuff my phone in my apron pocket, and slap on a cheery smile. "You didn't miss anything."

"He's not that bad." Arielle's peacock blue eyes trace the closed office door. "He's under a lot of pressure with the Coffee Loft and family stuff. Underneath this moody facade, he's got a heart of gold."

I sputter out a cough, then throw my fist in front of my mouth to fake another cough, covering up my ill reaction to her description of her brother. *Nobody with a heart of gold fires someone on Christmas Eve.* "You don't have to explain anything on his behalf."

"That's the thing." She unpacks the milk cartons, stowing them in the fridge. "I think I do. I'm not making excuses." She shakes her head as if she's rejecting shame. "What he did to you was terrible. I don't agree with it at all, and I intend to help him see that he was wrong. He's been in this hating people stage for a while." Lifting both shoulders up, she pauses while she takes a deep breath and exhales out the last part, "ever since our mother died."

"Oh." I pin a stoic expression on my face, unsure why I need to know about Christian's personal issues. I'm not insensitive, but it's clear we aren't friends. Still, I'm not one to be rude when someone is opening up to me. I keep the conversation going. "Sorry to hear that. Was it recent?"

"No." She pulls one side of her lips up into a disgruntled expression. "Like almost twenty years now. I barely remember her, and we each dealt with it differently. Seeing how short life was made me want to live life to the fullest. Christian had the opposite reaction, swearing off people. He'll never admit it, but it's an act. He's afraid to get close to anyone because he doesn't want to get hurt. I almost think the worse he treats someone, it's like an inverse barometer to gauge how much he could like you."

"Well, then he must love me," I sarcastically belt out, ready to laugh until my stomach hurt but Arielle's expression didn't waver from her serious one. "What?" I ask in my cynical tone.

"It's not love, but I definitely would say you have an effect on him."

Ice runs through my veins, and I sputter out another cough. I must be coming down with something. I didn't expect her to reply so thoughtfully, as I had been joking. Swallowing, as the mere suggestion of Christian not hating me made me queasy, I push the idea out of my head, redirecting my sights to the lobby.

Nobody here.

"Are you hungry?" Arielle shoves the grocery bag in the trash and pulls out her own phone. "Today has been crazy. I got Christian some pain meds. They'd be better on a full stomach. Can you stay for pizza if I order it? Christian's treat."

She paces to the office, cracks open the door all the while still scrolling on her phone. "You should treat us to some pizza since nobody ate today."

I don't see him from my spot behind the counter, but I can hear his forlorn reply. "That sounds like a terrible idea."

"You need to take some meds, and you shouldn't take those on an empty stomach."

"It won't be empty. I have two ketchup packets in my wallet I'm saving for tonight," he grumbles from behind the crack in the door.

I snicker and look away. I get he hurt his back *but come on!*

"Christian. This is important." Arielle steps inside the door, closing it almost all the way. Harsh whispers bicker back and forth until I hear Christian's gruff sigh.

"I *guess,* I can order pizza from that place across the street," he mutters. "It's just pizza. *And my sanity.*"

"I can run over there and grab it." Arielle offers as she tugs open the office door, heading out the exit before Christian has a chance to rebuttal. "I'll be back."

About half an hour later, Arielle returns with a single box of pizza. "I didn't realize that place closes so early. I got the last one." She sets the grease-soaked box on the counter. "I hope you like plain cheese, because that's all they had."

"That's fine." I'm so hungry I could eat the whole pizza myself, but I didn't tell her that.

She helps herself to plates and dishes out slices of pizza, handing one to me and then sets two more on a table, and calls out to Christian who is still locked up in his office. "Pizza's on the table!"

We stare at the door as it slowly creeps open, and Christian emerges with a polite nod to her while he hobbles over. "Tell me something." His gaze catches on mine. "Is this place always this dead?"

"Not when I worked." I stare at my pizza on the plate in front of me, waiting for him to connect the dots.

"Do you know what happened to my customers?" Christian lowers himself softly to the chair. I don't tell him that chair tends to be unstable. The old owner did nothing to repair this place.

"They might have been staying away after I told them you fired me."

"That's interesting." He shoots a stern look at Arielle, but she returns it even harder.

He lifts one foot with a quick jerking motion, plopping it on the chair in front of him as he folds his pizza in half like a true New Yorker, even though he's from Massachusetts. A cheese tail dangles in front of him as he breaks off his first bite. Drool puddles in my mouth, and I dig into my own slice.

After chewing, he dabs the corner of his mouth with a napkin and resumes conversation. "How did you contact them?"

I swallow my pizza and lick the dot of sauce that leaked onto my lip. "The old owner never had a system in place for ordering online. He's old school. I give my customers my number to text an order for pickup, and I *might* have replied back to all their messages letting them know I was fired."

"Hmm." His gaze zeroes in on me, while still shoveling pizza in the side of his mouth. Even in the dimly lit room, the silverish gray inflections in his eyes sparkle with honest interest. "You don't say." Christian finishes his last bite of pizza, picks up his second slice, and holds it in the air in pause while he talks. "So, do you think you can ask them to return?"

"I didn't tell them to leave. They just did that on their own."

With no change of expression, Christian drops his tone. "I'll be honest I assumed you did something to run them all off."

"That was all on them." I wanted so badly to bat my eyelashes the way I normally do when conversations get hard, but he is holding my gaze so steadily, I didn't dare flinch. "I'm really good at this job and they were being loyal."

Christian blinks a couple of times before his gaze slides to Arielle, who hasn't touched her pizza. She is typing on her phone. "El," he verbally pokes her. "You're the one who wanted the pizza, and you're not eating."

"What did you say?" Her top row of even teeth pinches her bottom lip. "I forgot we had food."

"That's my point exactly." Christian and I chuckle in unison as he jerks his thumb toward the door. "We'd better get out of here. It's getting late." He digs in his pocket, retrieving his key ring with a rental car tag still on it.

"Thanks for helping today!" Arielle smiles sweetly at me while grabbing the dishes we used and sliding them into the sink. She takes her untouched pizza off her plate, folding it in half, and biting it as she moves toward the door. "We'll see you again tomorrow. You are still going to open for me, right?"

"Sure." My phone vibrates, and I raise an eyebrow toward the screen.

Dad: They closed the interstate, but we pulled off in time to get one of the last hotel rooms. We are fine. Hope you are, too.

Rolling my bottom lip, I ponder. If Dad heard I went back to work here, he'd be concerned. They already have enough stress on their plate, and I didn't want to give them more stress. I text,

Me: That's too bad. Don't worry about me. Everything is fine.

I drop my phone in my pocket and look up, expecting to see the door shutting as they left in front of me. Instead, Christian is lingering behind with his eyes fixed on me. "Everything okay?"

"Yeah." My brows furrow together briefly. "Just my parents. They're supposed to drive home, but there's a weather delay. Nothing serious."

"That's too bad." He props the door open with his foot, not letting it close. "I noticed you walk here. Did you need a ride home?"

Normally, I'd say no because I like to hand out QR cards on my way home, but I'm anxious to get home fast to reply to all my messages. A ride would save me twenty minutes. "Yeah, I'll take one, if you're going that way."

"Come with us," Arielle waves me forward, and I pass through the door, falling in step with them.

"Thanks for dinner, by the way," I say to make conversation before adding, "That was nice of you." Alarmed, I check behind me. Where did that come from? Christian isn't nice. Those two words can never be in the same sentence. He's not capable of being nice. He's an incorrigible jerk I can't stand. I'm only here so Oliver doesn't get in trouble.

My brow bends slightly, not into a full furrow as I'm cautious about how my face flexes now that I'm almost thirty. I recall Arielle explaining Christian's mood is a guard.

Or is he nice?

Seventeen

Christian

I take the tiniest step, about to make a joke about my granny speed when my lips cringe into a pained wince. Everything about my situation is horrendous. I hate being in pain. I hate being weak. I hate relying on people to help me. "Sorry, I'm slow," I grumble. "This happens to my back sometimes."

Portia lingers behind me. "I'm sure you'll be okay."

I use all my strength to stand up straight as I have no desire to be vulnerable in front of her. This morning, she was doing everything she could to destroy my livelihood. She isn't my ally. I'm only being nice to her because I need her to train El.

I pace to my side of the car, climb in, crank the engine while El jumps in shotgun, and Portia crawls in back.

El reaches forward, rapidly switching the radio station, giving each station only a second to test before pressing the button again. It's something she's always done while I drive. It used to drive me into mocha madness, the way she pretended she owned my car. After not having spent much time with her this last year, it brings a wave of nostalgia. I miss spending time with her. She is quirky, doing things to bring me out of my need for control.

My nostalgia is short lived, lasting until she parks the setting on the latest hip-hop station and blasting back beats pound out of my speakers. Immediately, her duck lips glue to her face, and she bobs her head as if she is unsuccessfully trying to stretch a kink out of her neck. I shift the gear, pulling forward as the pressure in the back of my head swells. "Not happening." I push the "off" button and tighten my grip on the steering wheel. "I've had this headache for days, and that doesn't help."

She whistles, imitating a bomb being dropped.

"You have no idea the stress I'm under. I need some peace and quiet."

"You get enough quiet sitting at the Coffee Loft all day."

That stings, but I choose to ignore it. "Portia, what's your address?" I don't even glance in the rearview mirror as I wait for a reply from the backseat.

"I'm on Yellowstone Boulevard. Right around the corner from the Coffee Loft."

"Nice." I purse my lips in thought. I know the exact location. It's prime real estate next to the Long Island Railroad with plenty of commercial amenities, and a perfect view of Manhattan to the west. "Do you own?"

"Rent."

I glance at El. She's texting on her phone. Her chest rises gradually, falling even slower. Something's clearly up with her, but I'm not in the mood to talk. I drive forward.

"Right here." Portia points to a driveway after a few minutes, and I pull in, and jerk to a stop in the spot closest to the door.

I stare forward at the multilevel building and gamble with a guess. "Are you on the bottom floor?"

"Nope." She pops the P. "Tenth floor."

"Elevator?" My back twitches just thinking about all those steps.

"It's under construction." She props her door open and drops one foot on the pavement. "Thanks for the ride." Her voice softens, and she adds, "I hope you feel better."

I rub my eye. That's not what I expected to hear. Contrary to what Portia may think, I'm not a jerk, but I didn't think we were being that nice to each other. While dropping a heavy sigh, I force a smile. "Thank you."

Eighteen

Christian

I walk El inside the hotel, both hands stuffed in my pockets as I'm concerned about her. She's typing on her phone, and I see that dumb dating site open. "Chatting with random people on the internet is dangerous. You never know who you are talking to, especially since that site doesn't verify personal info. You'd better not be pretending to be me."

"It's fun." Her breezy laugh brushes away any concern. "I'm vetting the women for you. There really isn't much on there, but there's this one who has the same sense of humor as you."

"I didn't ask you to do that. It's dumb. Make your own profile if you love it so much."

Her voice dips off as her gaze focuses on the ground ahead of her feet. "I'm not ready for that."

Being nearly ten years apart in age, El and I never had the classic sibling rivalry of closely spaced siblings. When she was growing up, I always protected her. We talk honestly about everything. However, things had changed this last year with her at university. I get it. At some point you want to find your own way. I'm conservative, and she considers me, "too serious." I'm not going to pry. Instead, I offer encouragement. "So, you said before I don't need to beat anybody up. How about blackmail?"

She doesn't even twitch a smile. "Trust me, I've thought about it, but I don't think it will help."

"That's good you're keeping perspective. Do you think it'll help to give up on school?"

She emits a disgruntled sigh, but it doesn't shut down the conversation. "It seems like I quit school because of *him*, but it's really two separate things."

I'm still not sure what *him* she's talking about, but I don't interrupt. She continues, "If school had been right for me, I wouldn't have willingly ditched it so much. I don't see what the point of the expense is. At least for right now, I'd be happy working with you. If you need help at the Coffee Loft." She draws one side of her lips into an unconvincing smile.

A knot scratches at the back of my throat while I mentally inventory my bank account. It's easy to do because it's etched into my brain. A big fat zero balance. I'm starting to consider this Coffee Loft endeavor to be a mistake. I don't bother her with my concern. I reverse the focus back to her. "I finished college before I started this business. No matter what happens with my Coffee Loft, I can always fall back on my MBA. You need to have something to fall back on."

"See, that's where we're different." She holds up an index finger, injecting a point. "Unlike you, I have my good looks to fall back on."

Her dead-serious expression pins on her face, but I instantly crack into laughter. "You may have a point. Beauty over brains." I shake my head at this conversation. "I'm glad you learned the most important stuff while you were at school."

"It's important to explore all of your options, which is why I think you need to try this app—"

I clear my throat, and a sequence of tiny explosions ripples out. "Are you trying to upset me?"

"No, I'm trying to get you to lighten up, but apparently you hate fun."

"I don't hate fun. I don't have time for it." Sneering, I avoid looking at her. "I have responsibilities I can't run away from."

"I see." Her lips purse out while she quietly nods. "Now, we are passive-aggressively insulting."

"Was that passive aggressive?" I cocked my head toward her. "I'm sorry. I meant it to be direct."

"Woah!" She flashes her palm in my face in a stop motion. "Where is this coming from? All this built-up rage. Clearly, you need to do some sugar detoxing. Too much mocha in the mornings."

Determined not to let this conversation turn into a full-fledged argument, I raise my gaze to the heavens and release it. "I'm not arguing about this, El. We are two different people. I don't pressure you to live your life the way I think you should. I would appreciate the same respect."

"I get it," her voice treads softly. "You don't want to be told what to do."

"No, I don't," I affirm as strongly as I can, while we pass through the hotel lobby together. "Thanks for understanding."

"Okay, so what if instead of telling you what to do, I *suggest* something?" There's a distrustful hint of strange blue in her eyes, which I'd only ever seen when she was trying to frame me to get in trouble for something she did.

I narrow my gaze, proceeding with caution. "And what is it that you want to *suggest* I do?"

"For starters, I think you need to offer Portia her job back."

"What?" My eyebrow spikes, and my tone crescendos in annoyance.

"Don't make that face at me," El rushes. "You know I'm right."

"First, I'm not responsible for what my face does when I speak." I steel my face, trying to control it even though I know it's pointless. "And second, no. Why would I do that?"

"Well, to put it bluntly, you were a jerk to fire her at all, let alone at Christmas time, and you're barely managing to walk on two feet. You're really struggling. I don't mind helping, but she's a pro."

"El, it wasn't about me being nice, or a jerk, or whatever. You said it yourself: the Coffee Loft is dead quiet. Even if she was a lovely peach of a person, I don't have the business to keep her there. It was a business decision."

She points a finger gun at me. "Still a jerk, and didn't you notice your customers were her customers first. They will gladly line up to get coffee from her if they knew she's back."

"Who's to say she'd even come back?"

"She'll come back because you're going to beg her to."

I cough out a series of O's, tacking on at the end, "Oh, no, I won't."

"Look." She flicks her hand out in a gesture toward me as we walk into the elevator. "The way I see it, you don't have a choice."

"I fired her to get rid of her—"

"It's the only way." El touches my forearm, giving it a more than endearing squeeze. It was a sibling twist, that reverberated into my gut. "I think she's good for the store, and you need her."

"I thought that's why I had you." I wince as she continues to playfully twist my arm.

"Well, but you can't walk. Now I have the power, and I refuse to help until you make that relationship amiable." Dropping her arm back to her side, she now holds me in an eye lock, that hint of untrustable blue blazes at me. "Plus, she's not that bad. She has the same sarcastic sense of humor you have. If you'd give her a chance, and let that guard down a little, you'd like her."

"Like her? Now you've gone too far!" I snort, raising my chin as the elevator door opens, and I storm out, making a point. There's a bit of a raised ledge where the elevator floor meets the hotel floor, and I miss it, tripping hard. As I struggle to catch my fall, I twist into an expert contortionist move. It mostly works as I don't land on the floor. Except for the jolting pain shooting down my lower back into my tailbone, I'm fine.

"So, you agree." El tracks me like a bloodhound down the hall. "You'll make amends first thing tomorrow."

"I never said that."

"You didn't *not* say that."

"Right. I never *not* said that, but I also never said that, so please don't manipulate my words."

"Good. It's settled."

"Not settled."

"You should bring a gift, too." She taps her chin with her finger. "Something thoughtful."

I make it to our room and flash the keycard in front of the door. I wait for it to open, but the light doesn't shine. I swipe it two more times. "You need to go back to school to be a lawyer."

"We already talked about school. Remember, I'm helping you here."

"You're not being helpful." Finally, the green light flashes, and I'm in my room. It's been a grueling day, and I pace forward until my feet hit the edge of the bed.

She gives me *the* glare. Her secret sauce to get me to do things she wants me to do. Since she has the same almond-shaped eyes our mother had, it infuses my soul with enough guilt to work. She whispers, "Please."

Always a softy for her, I'm done. "Fine." I crash face first onto the pile of unmade blankets, and while El is still rambling on about that person I can't stand, I close my eyes. I'm so ready for this day to be over.

"Oh, Christian." El slides in next to me, pushing the phone close. "You must talk to this one. She's so funny."

"I'm not talking to anyone on that dumb site."

"Just this once, or I won't work in your store tomorrow."

"Is that blackmail?" I open one eye and confirm she's serious. "Fine." I hold out my palm, and she drops my phone in it.

Me: Heyyyyyy Profile 421! How are you? Fun fact. The more Ys people have in their greeting, the more interesting they are.

Profile 421: He

My head jerks back, and I snicker. That's so cheesy, it's funny.

"What do you want to reply back with?" El's leaning over me, reading the screen.

I push her away as I roll over and sit up. "I'm not showing you." I hover my thumbs over the screen and think. Something witty.

Me: Is there an airport nearby, or was that just my heart taking off?

Profile 421: That was an airplane. JFK. I heard it, too.

Me: So, you are on Long Island?

Profile 421: -es

I chuckle at the fact she's continuing to leave the Y out. She's clearly playful. I vow to make her slip up.

Me: Would you rather ride in a yacht, or camp on the yawn?

Profile 421: camp

I bleep out a chuckle, as that was too easy.

Me: Yogurt or Yams

Profile 421: Chocolate

Me: That isn't an option.

Profile 421: Chocolate is always an option.

Me: I got you to slip!!!! There's a y in always!!!!!

The screen flashes, and a message pops up.

You have successfully completed your chat. Do you vote to continue with this person?

Blinking, I come out of my trance. Somehow, I advanced a level. It's like a video game. I press, yes, and wait. It appears she's gone offline. Surprisingly a sting drops into my stomach as I feel a touch of disappointment. It's okay, though. I'm overtired, and I roll over on my stomach to sleep. *Only I don't sleep.* Oddly, I smile and ponder all the Y words I should have used.

The next day, I'm feeling a little better. Yet, I know from experience to take it easy and not jump back into activity. After resting all day, I'm going stir crazy and decide to drive over to pick El up from her closing shift at the Coffee Loft. Pretending I need to grab a deposit bag, I go inside. I don't have a deposit to make, unless we're talking about a bag to put my pride in. Even the bank bag is too big for the minuscule amount of pride I have left.

El walks behind the counter to shut off the espresso machines. I stroll through the lobby, turning off the lights.

When I reach the front of the store, I lock the door and inspect the street outside. People are everywhere, driving and walking to all the surrounding stores. Nobody is headed my way.

This place must be invisible.

Rubbing my eyes, hoping to bring some much-needed clarity, I turn back to find El handing me a coffee in a to-go cup. "What's this?" I take the cup while keeping my elbow straight, eyeing the cup from a full arm's length away.

"It's the almond milk, decaf, latte, but I swapped out your usual mocha for the sugar-free cinnamon dolce latte with an extra pump."

"Why would you swap out the sugar?" My voice screeches in horror. *Sugar is the best part!*

"Your mood, Christian. It's out of control." She wags her finger at my cup. "Less judgment. Just try it."

"There's nothing wrong with my mood. It's how I am. Coffee goes in, sarcasm comes out."

"The sarcasm is fine." Tilting her head toward me, she drops her voice as if someone might accidentally overhear, even though the place is empty. "It's that thing you do with your face."

I steel my jaw, resisting the urge to fight. My fingers are aflutter, but I raise my cup to my mouth and tip it back. Smooth. Surprisingly it's the perfect blend of sweet and cinnamon spice on the tip of my tongue, with a rich coffee aftertaste. *So good.* I take an extra swallow because I don't want the taste to stop. When I come up for air, El has her sus glint in her eye again. "What?"

"Somebody was here on behalf of the Chamber of Commerce, selling tickets to a fundraising dinner. I bought us tickets."

"Why?"

"What do you mean why?" Her blinks fire off in rapid succession. "You have no customers, and you are invited to a business social event. You're desperate. So, you go."

"That sounds like the kind of thing you like to attend." I swipe my hand through my hair, not caring that it didn't even tame my front spike. "You can go."

"I can go." She affirmed with a curt nod. "But so can you. It's your business that's failing."

"Thanks for the encouragement." When she doesn't defend her stupid dinner again, I know the glint was about *that other thing*. It's clearly the glint of doom, confirmed by her flashing a look at her smart watch. "We need to run along. It's getting late, and Portia might be going to bed soon." She retrieves another cup from the counter, one with a to-go sticker over the drink hole. "For Portia."

"I'm not giving her free coffee," I mutter, staring at the cup as if it will bite me. "Perhaps I need to explain what running a business is about. You SELL things to make money. If you give away more than you sell, you go broke."

She pushes the cup closer until almost touching my stomach. I take a step of rejection back. "I need to go to the bank."

"You *need* to bring her a gift, too." She floats the drink closer to me, brushing it against my arm, like a giant delicious fly. "Remember, she gets her job back, too."

I narrow my gaze. "You're such a traitor, El."

"It's the only way out of this mess." She dramatically scans the room. "You have no customers until she returns, because they are clearly following her. When she was here, it was busy. Now that she is gone, it's dead." She slowly waves the cup in front of my face like a pendulum she's using to hypnotize me.

I disgruntledly accept the cup from her hand, and spin on my heel. I didn't want to say El made me take it because that makes me look weak—like my little sister controls me—which she clearly doesn't. "Fine. I'll bring her a present, but she's not getting her job back. I'll get her to call off this war *my way*."

Fifteen minutes later, I'm holding Portia's coffee and a plastic grocery sack of almost stale Oreos I'm about to throw out from the Coffee Loft. I brace my lower back with my free hand as I hobble up the cement stairs to Portia's apartment. This isn't even my apartment, but I'm about to call the building manager to complain about the broken elevator. It's a real inconvenience.

About the Oreos. They aren't exactly a "present," as El had tried to force me to bring to Portia. It's me hating to see my money go in the trash, and I can't stand Oreos enough to eat them myself. My aversion is due to the fact when I was little my grandma forced me to eat the last stale one after getting over the flu. I was barely even able to keep anything down. She gave me one, threatening me not to waste the cookies I forced her to buy me, all while standing over me until I ate the whole thing. Gagging, I stop myself from dry-heaving at the memory, and force my brain to the present. *El is out of her mind to think I'll bring Portia a real present. As if I owe her anything after she stole all my customers.*

"So, ten flights of stairs, huh?"

"Yep," El quips as she bounces joyfully up each stair.

"What is she, Rapunzel?" I grunt and dig deep into my core as I put one foot in front of the other, making it up the first flight with *ease.* The uneasy part came on the next flight, where I sucked in so much air I should have floated up. Turns out, it doesn't work like that. All that air inhaled, and I'm not any lighter.

This is absurd.

Did we get invited?

Nope.

Do I feel super weird?

Yes.

"I'm sure she's resting," I argue, completely annoyed El convinced me to come here.

"I told her we'll stop over." She pulls her ash blonde hair back over her shoulder and looks back at me. "I think you two need to talk things out."

"Almost there," I grunt out, rounding the last corner of the final set of stairs. I clearly need to work out more. In times like this, my lack of athleticism is a tad embarrassing. In my defense, I wasn't warned. I struggle between holding my breath and pulling in so much air, that I sound like a plugged vacuum. "Here!" I pant out as soon as my foot crests the top step. "We made it." I brace my hands above my knees and breathe. *Oh man. Life is so good when you are on flat land.* I trudge forward, leading the way to Portia's apartment door, lifting my fist to knock. I plan to knock so lightly that there's no way she hears us. I'll confirm she's sleeping, and we can leave.

It's a genius plan.

I reach her door and lightly scratch on the surface while holding my breath. *Well, looks like no one is home, or she's resting.* I hook the bag of Oreos on the doorknob, and set the cup in front of the door, careful not to make even the slightest peep. Snickering about how lucky I am that she didn't hear me, I tiptoe toward the steps. This is too easy. Now, to make it down the stairs. I slide my toes down the first stair, a sly smile growing on my face while I brace my back again.

I made the mistake of not checking my blind spot and out of the corner of my eye I see El is not following me, but rather, she's loudly pounding on the door. "Portia! Are you still awake!"

"Shh!" My hands curl into fists, and they shake as I pivot and scowl at her. "You're going to wake her with all that noise!"

As soon as the door cracks, I'm greeted by someone. Well, let's call it a some*beast.* A giant dog heaves across the hall, knocking over the coffee, only to pop off the lid, spilling it. He doesn't slow until he jumps on me and licks my cheek. He's friendly. That's amazing. "Ah, you have a dog." Struggling to hold him off me, I pinch my lips together as it won't take long for my allergies to kick in. As I push him off, I recognize him to be the same beast who broke my back, and I tense up.

"Oh, shoot, Oliver!" Portia lunges forward, grabbing his collar, but he barks rapidly trying to free himself from her grasp. I barely hear her explain over the barking, "I walked him, and his owner isn't home again. I'm holding him here until she gets back. This is so unlike him. He normally doesn't approach anyone unless I direct him too."

"Shreeeeeek!" A horrendous squealing noise wails from inside her apartment, and we all pivot to look inside. Portia leans in, quirking an eyebrow, quickly scanning inside. Panic reflects in her eyes. "Mr. Noodles is gone!" She spins in a circle, but when that doesn't bring her relief, she runs to the window. It's cracked at the bottom; the linen curtain blows slightly from the light breeze. "Oliver!" She calls as her head whips in all directions, scanning the street. "Your barking scared Mr. Noodles into jumping out of the window! He's running down the fire escape, and he's headed into traffic! We have to get him."

I don't even know who Mr. Noodles is. Apparently, Oliver does, because as soon as Portia accuses him, he turns his gaze, refusing to engage Portia. "Look at that." She aims her finger toward him as he cowers against the wall. "He knows he's guilty."

"He sure does look guilty." I fight the urge to slide my foot back. This is turning into a bit of a circus. I don't have time to look for Mr. Noodles. I don't even know what that is. Oh boy, she has tears in her eyes. "It's f-fine." I stutter out. "He'll fly back."

"He's not a bird," she sniffs out. "It's my cat. He's been with me ever since I moved out on my own. He's not an outside cat. He can't survive out there." Her shoulders tremble, resembling dainty hiccups.

"Oh, no!" El's mouth drops open. "He could die! We have to find him." She's staring at me with our mother's eyes, and it makes my gut wrench. Before I talk some sense into myself, I open my big, fat mouth. "Let's all split up, and everybody search."

What did I just say?

It echoes in my head, taunting me like a dare I gave myself.

How am I going to find a cat?

I don't even know what he looks like. It's dark out.

This woman makes my blood boil.

Now I'm going to waste my time looking for a dumb cat?

How about I tape my mouth shut instead?

That would be better than this!

"Are you sure?" Portia's gaze cements on mine—hope buds in her irises. "I feel bad. Are you even feeling better?"

"Suuuure." My voice pitches higher at the end as I mentally prepare for what I'm about to do. "It's not a problem. Let's keep the dog here so he doesn't scare it away again." I motion inside, and glare at the beast and catch sight of something on the nightstand. A 5x7 framed photo of a gray cat and her. *Oh, adorbs. A cat selfie, I sarcastically say in my head. And she framed it.* I study the creature. Gray. Cat. Whiskers. Like every gray cat with whiskers. "This should be . . . be really easy." I can't get whole sentences out, as I'm so furious with myself for volunteering, but it's late and she's crying. I can't handle when a woman cries. I glare at El. "You coming?"

"I'll head west, you go east."

"I'll go south." Portia pulls the door closed behind her as she's already heading down the stairs.

"*Sweeeell.*" I force my lips into a toothy grin. "I better get going too. It *is* rather late." I screech, the highest octave my voice has ever hit. I'm a bit amazed I even have that range. *It's clearly a hidden talent I didn't even know I had. I could totally take on one of those singing competition shows and win the whole thing. Then I can give up my failed Coffee Loft, living the dream on a yacht in the Caribbean—*

"Christian," her soft voice cuts my daydream spiral off, pulling me back to her.

I was afraid to ask, but against my better judgment I whispered out in fear. "What do you need?"

"Thank you." The tiniest smile curls on her lips. It is the first genuine smile I've seen on her face, and I can't stop staring at it. Her lips are cotton candy pink. A dimple sits right above her chin. A perfect little button of happiness— *What is wrong with me?* I jolt my head back, shaking myself out of this insanity. It's already been a loooong day.

"Yeah, whatever," I grumble as I wave goodbye and struggle to keep pace with her while descending the steps. "Don't worry about anything. One of us must find him."

Portia took off way ahead of me, but left me with a burning image in my brain of her smiling. Her soft blonde waves frame her face. *She is stunning.*

When did that happen?

Feeling a tad feverish, I fan my face and cross the hall. "Great. Now, I'm coming down with something." *Clearly, my stress is making me ill.*

Or is it . . .

Nineteen

Portia

I received a text from Christian saying he had found Mr. Noodles, and I ran home at record speed to meet him. He's seriously slow because both Arielle and I beat him to my apartment and made hot chocolate by the time he hobbled up. A single knock sounds on the door, and I whip it open.

"I got your cat," he grumbles. "Now, give me Arielle, and we can leave."

My jaw plummets. He has deep rows of scratches etched into both sides of his face, mimicking sideburns. I size them to match the exact width of Mr. Noodles' claws. Mud cakes his pants all the way up to his knees. I can't even tell what color his shoes are. Mr. Noodles is wrapped in his jacket, and tucked in a ball under his arm with a scowl, clearly unhappy.

"That's not my cat, by the way." Blinking, I tease him. "You can put him back from wherever you got him."

"Not your cat!" he screeches as his face grows scarlet. "I don't care if it's not your cat. He is now. He's gray. He has whiskers. He was in a tree right across the street. I climbed the tree, but he fled before I could grab him. Then I chased him down a muddy alley, all while slipping and sliding to my death. I finally cornered him between a building and a trash can. I had to use my good jacket to restrain him but not before he ripped my face off. I'm not putting him back. I didn't want to agree to any of this." He reaches his hands out, dangling the cat out in front of him. "I'm done!"

Clumsily catching Mr. Noodles, I cradle him next to my chest, and he curls right in. I'm not mean. Christian went through the hassle of finding Mr. Noodles, and I can tell he doesn't think this is funny. "It's my cat. I was joking. Sorry, if that stressed you out more."

"Good!" He bobbles his head while parking both hands on his hips. "I'll leave you two alone then."

"Thank you for everything." My words rush out a little garbled up, and I hope they aren't lost.

He sticks his head into my door, calling out, "El, it's time to leave."

She glides across the room and smiles at me. "Christian needs to talk to you before we leave." She glares at him. "Right?"

Christian clamps down on his bottom lip, pausing for an insanely long time. I actually toss a look back to Arielle to make sure I understood her, but she only nods back to Christian. Finally, when I'm assuming, Christian lost his voice, he burps out, "Do you want your job back?"

Arielle elbows him on the arm. He snorts, pinching his lips together tightly, but sputters out, "*Please.*"

I bat my eyes. "I'd love that."

"Great, have a nice night with Mr. Murder Claws." He turns on his heel and heads straight for the stairs.

"Night." Arielle flashes a wave at me as she pinches back a smile and follows him.

Snuggling Mr. Noodles in my chest tighter, I press a kiss to the top of his head as I shut the door, and head back to my futon, chuckling.

TWENTY

Christian

With my hands shoved in my coat, I march up the sidewalk to my store, slowing right before I reach the door. *There are people inside!* I can see them through the window. Not just a couple of people, either. I jerk open the door and plow in, scanning the rows of tables, all filled with customers already served.

It's the very next day after I struck that truce with Portia. I struggle to open my eyes wider, taking long strides to the bar where Portia's steaming milk, a row of six to-go cups lined up ready to fill. Her hair is up in a messy bun on top of her head. She also has a funky wrap headband thing tied around her head. Festive snowflake earrings dangle from each ear, and she has a full smile on her face as she greets me. "Good morning, Christian."

My eyes scan the messy counter dotted with drips of milk in random places and a small pile of spilled coffee grounds underneath the grinder. In the corner, the trash is nearly overflowing with empty milk containers, all evidence she hasn't had even a small break in traffic. Normally, I loathe mess, and hate clutter. After days of everything being nothing but shiny clean, this mess is the most beautiful thing I've ever seen.

Mess means money! Portia standing in the middle of the mess makes her the most beautiful woman I've ever seen. "What did you do?"

"I sent a text to all my clients, inviting them back." Portia reaches forward, grabs the mocha sauce and pumps it into a cup. "I explained everything was a mix-up."

I'm at a loss for words. These really are my customers. El was right about bringing Portia back. She brought all my people back with her. A man in a business suit walks up to the counter, his face beaming at Portia. "Glad to see you back," he greets her.

"Good to see you, too, Trey." She beams at him, while adding lids to all the cups, and setting them on the bar for customers waiting off to the side. "Do you want your usual?" she asks over her shoulder, while she grabs the last two cups and places them on the counter for pickup.

"Yeah, please."

I stand back as she goes to the tablet, punching in his order without confirming what it is. He opens his wallet, pulls out a ten-dollar bill, and doesn't wait for change. It's the most beautiful thing I've seen since I arrived.

The door opens and more people file in, lining up. My eyes well with happy tears as I honestly was doubting there were people in this town who drank coffee. What I didn't see was their loyalty to Portia. They hadn't had time to get to know me, or my Coffee Loft.

I thought I had to do this all on my own, building up my dream store. I almost missed out on the best gift of all. Portia is a customer service ninja, taking orders with one hand while waving goodbye to happy customers with the other, calling them all by their first names. I stumble behind her, inserting myself into the happy chaos, ready to fill her orders.

We say nothing about the past awkwardness as we fall into an orderly rhythm of her taking orders, and me making the coffees, all while the traffic pours through the door all morning. It's after eleven before we get our first lull, and I'm able to take two full bags of trash outside. Hugging the bags close to my chest as if they are loving pets, I've never been so happy to haul trash out in my life. I'm humming gleefully on my way back inside, right as Portia unties her apron and stuffs it in the laundry bin.

Dirty aprons and rags! Another delightful sight I want to cry out to heaven in gratitude. It all means I'm finally making money. "That's it for my shift." She grabs the

stuffed tip jar and dumps it on the counter, quickly counting the money into two piles.

"Take it all." I place my hand on the pile closest to me
and scoot it all into the other pile. "I don't deserve any of
this."

She hikes a brow while her hand hovers over the un-
counted money. "Are you sure?"

"Yeah, I am." Usually I'm stubborn to admit my mis-
takes, but I'm so ecstatic to finally see customers that I
don't hold back. "I'm truly sorry about everything, and
I'm grateful you gave me a second chance."

She scoots all the money off the counter, stacking the
bills neatly into a pile. I'm a little jealous as I see a few
twenties flash, and by the height of that pile, it looks like
it could pay a few bills. Clearly, her customers came out in
droves to support her. Humbled, I stay mute as she finishes
stowing her money and returns the empty jar to its spot on
the bar.

"Arielle gave me part of her morning shift tomorrow,
too. Apparently, she's not a morning person, so I'll see you
then." She pivots, aiming for the door.

Before I know what I'm doing, I call out, "Wait a
minute."

She does the look back. The one you see on hair commercials. With her hair piled high on her head, a few fallen
strands framing her face, and she perks a feather bold eyebrow. "What do you need?"

"Ah, just to thank you."

Her lips curl into a brilliant, sassy grin, laced with the perfect balance of joy and attitude. "The pleasure is all mine." When she spins on her heel, I'm left with the impact of her smile, sending aftershocks right to my heart. I grab my chest and press my hand over my heart to steady it's pounding beats. What is going on?

Maybe El is right about needing to switch to sugar-free lattes? Clearly, this is medical and has nothing to do with Portia.

TWENTY-ONE

Portia

It's nice to have cash in my pocket again, and a work schedule to secure even more. I love the idea of being self-employed with my own match-making business. After this last test run, I'm positive I'm not ready to pull the trigger all the way yet. The website needs more organic growth to sustain steady traffic, and not require full-time recruiting. Until I get to that point, I will proudly wear my Coffee Loft apron.

It's my second opening shift after returning to work. Today is as crazy as yesterday, bringing a steady, enjoyable, fleet of customers. I had also switched the Coffee Shop satellite station back to Christmas music, and that is putting me in the best mood. I'm one of those people who can listen to Christmas music all year round. Since it is still December, with New Year's Eve being tomorrow, I'm going to enjoy all my favorites while I can get away with it.

Humming away, I shine the counters as Christian walks through the front door, an urgency in his stride. His gaze paces the room with a few scattered customers sitting in their booths. A pleased grin grows on his face as he continues to saunter to the back. "Good morning."

"Good morning." I exude a cheery tone after yesterday went off without a hitch, and I consider friendship *possible*. "I thought Arielle was coming in this morning."

"She was supposed to, but she woke up in the middle of the night with some stomach bug. I told her to rest." He scans over my workspace, everything a whole lot tidier than it was yesterday. "Is everything okay?"

"Yeah, it's been great. Steady but not too much that I can't keep up." I jerk my thumb over my shoulder to the back freezer. "I pulled milks already, and everything up here is ready for your shift. Oh!" I hold my hand up, interrupting myself. "Before I forget, you need to add Oreos to your grocery list. I searched all over the last two days, and the pantry is bare."

"Duly noted." His expression is neutral but his gaze slides to my overflowing tip jar on the counter. "Boy, Portia, I'd say you win the tip contest. I've never seen a more crammed jar after a morning rush. How do you do it? Money sure loves you."

I lift my shoulders into a modest shrug. "My dad always says you get what you give. I consider the tips a gauge in how much care I give others."

"You are amazing with people." He walks to the hand-washing station and starts pumping soap out of the wall dispenser onto his hand. "So anyway, I have a small issue with El being sick. There's this business after-hours thing on the last Friday of every month. El signed us up and bought two tickets. I guess it's a lot of walking around, and sipping wine while handing out business cards. Since it's between the holidays this month, the chamber organized a charity fundraiser dinner thing instead of the usual business promotion. Honestly, I hate these kinds of things. They are too peoply. But since I'm new to the area, I think she might be right that I need to meet people in town, especially other business owners. Uh, so I'm, uh, thinking."

He stops talking but is still pumping soap. A whole pile of foam engulfs his hand as he evidently isn't paying attention to what he's doing. I giggle as the tower wavers. It's the leaning tower of Palmolive. Likely it's Soft Soap but I was going for the P word. Leaning tower of Soft Soap doesn't have the same ring. Or worse yet, knowing Christian's cheap self, it's a store brand and that would sound even worse.

"So, I hate those people things. I guess, I already said that, but, uh, would you want to go to it, too? You seem like you'll enjoy that sort of thing." Instead of looking at me, he startles as he finally notices the mountain of soap on his hand and quickly turns on the water to rinse it down. It's extra foamy soap, bubbling into a swollen mass that looks as if it's coming alive. He pretends not to notice the bubble plume rise as he shakes the water off his hands. "Of course, you'll get paid. It's a work thing."

"A people event, huh?" Pinching my lips together to stifle my giggles, I force my gaze from the still rising soapsuds, and take my tip jar to sort through my money into a neat pile. Out of the corner of my eye, I see he's splashing water on the bubbles, hopelessly trying to wash them down the drain, but they continue to swell. "Do I get overtime pay?"

"Ah, sure." He clicks his heels together, standing up straight next to the soap pile, his eyes not acknowledging anything amiss.

I can't hold it back anymore and I burst out laughing. "What are you doing?"

Nervous laughter trickles from his lips, and he squawks, "These bubbles have a mind of their own!"

"Only because you pumped the whole bottle! You were completely zoned out." I chuckle again, enjoying how easy it is to joke with him today. "You almost need a mop bucket." I reset my tip jar, stuffing my money into my purse, keeping my gaze low. "What time is the dinner?"

"Ah, the social is at five. I'll shut the doors a little early here."

I strap my purse on my shoulder and take a few strides toward the door. As I push the door open, I flash back a smile. "You know where to pick me up." I catch his expression right as he absorbs my words and his lips bend into a winning smile.

I proceed to stroll through the door, and enter the rare winter sunshine, analyzing what happened. I get that Christian is wanting help for his event, but he wouldn't ask me to go if he still hated me, right? And if he didn't want to hang out with me, he'd probably pay me to go *without* him. Maybe I'm reading into this a little too much, but when I think about how awkward he was when he asked, he was nervous. A quibble bubbles in my gut. Why would he be nervous unless he cared how I'd reply?

My phone vibrates in my coat pocket, and I pull it out. "Hey, Dad."

"Sweetheart, how are you?"

"Good, actually." I walk briskly at a New Yorker's pace down the sidewalk toward my apartment. "I got my job back at the Coffee Loft, and finished a shift."

"See?" He chuckles his good-natured laugh. "I knew that loser would come to his senses."

"Tell me you guys are finally home safe?"

"We are home and ready to report for duty. Do you want to go to the Home Hardware tonight?"

"I would, but I can't. Christian asked me to do this charity fundraiser dinner for work."

"Interesting. Boy, it seems that Christian fellow changed his tune, giving you your job back, and having you do this. What do you think changed?"

I trap my bottom lip with my teeth, weighing the option to confess what happened. Now that Dad is home safe, I don't see a reason to hide the truth anymore. "Well, it is sort of weird, but Oliver jumped on him the other day, and made him fall down the subway. I didn't want to bother you with the stress while you were trapped out of town. Christian spent a couple of days laid up, and I didn't want Oliver to get in trouble, so I helped. I think we both realized we got off to a bad start. So, yeah, and so far, it's . . ."

I pause giving Dad time to chime in, but he is quiet, so I say, "Dad, you still there?"

"I'm here." He huffs into the phone. "Sounds suspicious."

"It's not sus. His business is failing since I took all his customers, and like I said, we're starting over."

"That's not how things usually work."

"What do you mean?"

"He's up to something. Playing a game, or he likes you. I'm going to have to meet him. Do you work tomorrow?"

"Dad," I rush to cut him off. "You're always welcome to visit me, but there's no reason you need to meet him, other than he's my boss." My cheeks heat, despite my denial.

"You didn't answer my question. Do you work tomor-row?"

"I close, so I'll be there until seven."

"Then I will, too."

"Dad—"

"Love you."

I flash my eyes heavenward and blow out a breath. "Love you, too." He'd already ended the call. I stuff my phone back into my coat pocket, focusing on my walk with a new smile on my face. What if Dad is right?

TWENTY-TWO
Christian

I hike the stairs to Portia's apartment with frustration over her broken elevator simmering up. I don't even live in this building, and I'm about to start looking for a new apartment. This is getting ridiculous. I brace my still-tender lower back and slay another flight.

Something is going on with my chest. It started on the drive over here. Adrenaline surged and it's been hours since my last coffee. Despite my attempts to practice measured breathing, my heart rate won't slow. Evidently, the stress of the last few days has now given me a heart condition.

I stop on the top landing, supporting my hands above my knees, panting. This must be the *last time* I climb those stairs to Portia's Rapunzel tower. I adjust my jacket collar to let in some air. It's supposed to be a nice night for December, staying way above freezing. I hadn't packed much other than work clothes when I arrived on Long Island. I knew I wouldn't have space to store anything, nor did I have plans to do anything but work. Something told me a Coffee Loft apron isn't appropriate for this event. I managed to find a red-collared shirt at a clothing store down the street, and it only set me back forty-five bucks. I hate spending money on clothes, or rather anything other than my bills, but I did it. I smooth down the front, before resuming my route to Portia's apartment, knocking firmly on the wood door.

Portia appears, wearing a smokey blue dress that sets off a fire of blue sparkles in her eyes. Now that she is not glaring at me about a missing French press, I find her eyes enjoyable to look into. No words are needed from me. I'm fine, just standing here.

"Hey, you." Portia's lips are accentuated by a rosy lip shade, a color she doesn't wear to the Coffee Loft. She pins on a grin. This isn't her malicious smile, the one that despises me, or her forced one. This one lingers, setting off another series of sparkles in her eyes, making it feel extra special—like a *date* smile.

"Hey." I prop one hand on the door frame, leaning in. I hadn't asked her to come for any other reason than to help me network, but with the way she's looking at me . . .

"How's it going?" I wince as I should say something more charming than that!

"Good." She passes through the door, locking it behind her, and we set off together back down the stairs.

"I'm getting in great shape from running up and down these stairs," I say, easing into conversation.

"It's been an adjustment." One of her hands slides down the rail while the other secures a petite clutch in front of her. "But actually, I did see guys working on the elevator today. Maybe if everything goes well, I'll have a functioning elevator before I need a walker."

"I'm ready to complain for you. I'll keep my fingers crossed that it's completed soon." We round the first landing of stairs and start on the next flight. I'm trying hard not to support my back as I don't want to look weak in front of her. Actually, it's a lot better than it was a few days ago. Things are looking up.

Now, if I can meet the right people tonight, maybe even some event coordinators, who can become regular clients for large catering, I can start to get my name out there. That will be perfect.

"You seem to be feeling much better." She keeps the conversation rolling.

"Yes." I give a nod. "The first day was the absolute worst, but each day has been better, and now I barely even notice it except for a few random spasms."

We settle into a comfortable silence as I descend the stairs one stair above her, counting off each flight in my head. When we reach my car, she rushes to open the door for herself. It's a tad awkward as this isn't a date, but my mother raised me right, and I prefer to do that for her. I stand back, waiting for her to lift her feet inside the car, and close the door. Then I hop in my side of the car, crank the engine, and pull onto the road.

"Was it busy after I left the shop?" Portia leans on the door armrest, taking an angled look back at me.

"Not too bad. I had a few larger tables, and they kept me busy. Since you had everything stocked, there wasn't much to do. I locked up early and called to check on El. She's okay, for having the flu."

"I love how you call her El." She gestures toward me casually. "I sort of want to do that, too, but she hasn't said it's okay. Is it an exclusive nickname?"

"I don't think exclusive nicknames are a thing. It's what she's always been to me."

"Interesting." She purses her lips, but I can tell she's not done with the questions. Women never are. "You two seem close," she adds.

"We can be." I grip the steering wheel tighter, pondering how much of my personal life I want to tell her. The thing is, El is chatty, the kind of person who has never met a stranger. I assume El had already told Portia my entire life story. That's the one thing I hate about El. There're always two sides to every pancake, and she only ever shares her side. Sometimes she doesn't paint me in the best light. "I don't know how much El's told you, but we mostly had our dad and grandmother to raise us. Dad worked in our family construction business with my grandparents, so we all were together a lot."

"I don't recall the family business mentioned. That almost sounds like an ideal childhood, in some ways."

"Don't get me wrong, I'm glad I had that experience, but I always knew it wasn't something I wanted to do with my life. There's been a lot of drama since I chose Coffee Loft as a career. But then again," I shrug, new tension pooling in the back of my neck from the mere thought of my family, "Isn't there always drama with family?"

"Not for me." Portia's eyes light up. "My parents are my rock, especially my dad. He is overly supportive of me." She giggles, covering her mouth with her hand before finally leaking out, "There's no secret that I'm his princess. He'll do anything for me. It was his idea for me to come back and hang out in front of your Coffee Loft after I got fired."

"I do have to hand it to you." I hold up a finger. "As much as I hated you at that moment, looking back, it is quite funny."

She chuckles deviously, her chin lowering. "I only wish I could have gotten your facial expression on video."

"I'm sure it was masterful." I smash my lips together, forcing a serious expression, but it is useless. Inside, I'm dying to share a cathartic laugh after the week I had. I allow a short, sarcastic scoff. I pull into a parking space behind the venue and kill the engine.

Normally, I'd hop out and be all business, but something about the laughter in the car makes me pause. I focus directly on her. "Look at us laughing together. Can you believe we rode in a car together and nobody died?"

"Don't celebrate yet." She laughs an airy flutter before pulling her door handle. "The night is still young."

I swallow, a mixture of anticipation, dread and, oddly, excitement all swirling together in my chest. One thing is for sure, I have no idea what tonight will bring.

TWENTY-THREE

Portia

My fingers nervously touch my collarbone as if I'm clutching an invisible string of pearls, while Christian leads me inside the convention room. A winter wonderland greets us, lining a red-carpet walkway with Christmas trees—dotted with sparkling gold lights. A couple dressed in high-society designer labels, with magazine-ready smiles, stand by the entrance, greeting everyone and scanning tickets.

I'm not usually a self-conscious person. Dad had always insisted nobody was better than anybody, drilling that into my head from the time I was young, but I stiffen and instantly feel underdressed. Dragging my feet, I linger back as Christian pulls out his phone, presenting his tickets to the man to be scanned.

When Christian pauses to stow his phone in his pocket, he notices I'm not standing beside him. His brow hikes north. "What's wrong?"

I had assumed this was nothing more than some casual spaghetti dinner thing, and I don't want to be disrespectful. Concealing my mouth with my palm, I whisper, "I should have guessed by the rows of BMWs in the parking lot but I'm feeling a little underdressed for this."

"Don't." His brows lower into a stern expression, and his voice deepens. "You look perfect."

Blinking, I absorb his compliment, feeling it deep in my gut. We inch forward, my trepidation simmers, and I case the room filled with people. All the women are adorned with full ball gowns, in either a festive red or black satin. I'm glowing in a bad way in my blue day dress. "Relax," Christian whispers to me.

I plaster on a smile and edge further into the room. "What am I doing wrong?"

"You're not doing anything wrong, except you look terrified."

I feel terrified.

But I can't admit that.

"I prefer to blend in better."

Nodding toward the doorway, he whispers, "Do you want to leave?"

I'm painfully pining for the exit, but I somehow manage to stutter out, "N-No. We can't do that. You bought those crazy expensive fundraising priced tickets, and we just got here. You need to meet some people."

He takes a step closer, nearly brushing my side as he speaks softly. "If you're uncomfortable here, I don't want to stay."

"It's weird," I speak slowly, surprised I'm confessing my true feelings instead of pretending to be brave. "I'm an expert with people when I'm in my element. Give me a hardware store, or the park, and I never even crack a nerve, but this feels . . ." I blow out a breath, unable to finish my thought as my gaze fixes on a row of model-tall women, all lined up in dresses that were more than likely worth more than all my earthly possessions combined. I search for something to soothe me. Opera music plays in the background, and everybody is eating and drinking with their pinky fingers jutting out. It's so proper—not at all my scene. "Phew. I've never been socially anxious before."

"It stinks. Trust me. It's why I hate these things."

"Here, I thought I was going to be helpful to you." I cringe into an "I'm-sorry smile" and shift my weight from one heel to the other. "Can I tell you the truth?"

"Sure."

"I sort of hate it here already."

Christian's lips spread into a genuine grin. "Did we actually find something we agree on?"

"I think so." I rush to agree, still clutching my imaginary pearls. "Let's bail fast before someone sees us."

Christian scans the room once more, not looking at all disappointed before holding out his arm for me to latch onto. "Let's bust out of this place."

I tuck my arm into his, allowing him to properly escort me out. "Where are we going?" I whisper out of the side of my mouth. Being this close to him brings a whiff of his aftershave that hints of a sea crusted breeze, making me feel lighter on my toes.

"I feel bad I dragged you out, and you didn't even get anything to eat." He tugs on my arm, pulling me faster the closer we get to the door. "I already paid for two hours of parking. What do you say we walk around the block? I saw an Irish pub on the way."

"Sounds good to me." We round the corner in the hall, taking a wrong turn. Instead of finding the hotel exit, we stumble across another event room. A cheery arch of gold and burgundy balloons frames the doorway and laughter wafts from inside the vibrantly lit room. Slowing as we pass in front of the door, I peek inside, and spot a three-tiered cake on a head table with a 'Happy Birthday, Pappi!' gold banner above it.

"That looks cute." I nod toward the room as a lady walks out. She's dressed in her Sunday best, a modest dress, and heels to match. Her hair is piled high into a Marge Simpson bun, and her shining eyes round when they find me. "Alisa! We've been waiting for you."

"Ah." I startle into a stillness. "I'm sorry, you have the wrong person."

She places a hand on my arm, leaning into my ear, and whispers, "I know you aren't Alisa. But please, please, please, if you have any spec of a human heart and ten minutes, can you go along with it? It's my grandpa's birthday, and he's sitting here waiting for his favorite granddaughter. He has dementia and doesn't remember she ran off with her boyfriend. She hasn't spoken to anyone in the family for a year. Please, just give us ten minutes." She folds her hands in prayer, pleading. "I'm afraid he's about to cry. He has terminal cancer, with only months to live, and we want so badly for him to enjoy his party. He refuses until he sees Alisa."

"Ah." I part my lips, feeling how dry they are in the stale air while I glance at Christian.

He offers an encouraging shrug. Talk about shoulders. I love it when he does that. "We don't have anything else to do."

"Okaaay." I take a few steps forward while smoothing my hair. "Do I look all right? What should I say?"

"He's nearly blind. It doesn't really matter what you look like." She extends her arm, ushering me inside the room. "By the way, my name's Ashley and we're best friends and cousins. Just be sure to call him Pappi, and maybe joke about how he eats too much ice cream."

"I can do that." As this feels a lot like my recruiting skit, I place my recruiting smile on my face and toss a glance at Christian, all the while my heart breaks as I think about this poor man not understanding why his favorite grandchild isn't there on his special day.

"Oh, he can come." Ashley waves him forward. "He's too cute to leave in the hall. Help yourself to some food. Please, make yourself comfortable. This means so much to me."

The three of us enter, simultaneously skirting along the edge of the room until we make it to the head table. A little man with a silver beard and a few long strands of a matching combover, partially concealing a shiny head, hunches over in his chair. His dull gray eyes, devoid of any sparks, stare forward with a forlorn expression.

"Pappi, look who I found outside," Ashley calls out, sparking the man to look our way. As soon as he sees me, his eyes fire a spark of light.

"Alisa!" He reaches forward, waiting for a hug. All the eyes in the room are on me, but nobody moves to act as if I'm out of place. I lean in, giving Pappi a big squeeze. His scent, a mixture of black licorice and oregano, wafts up my nose while I lightly pat his back until I pull away.

A tear buds in the corner of his eyes, and even though I've just met this man, my smile is genuine. "Happy birthday, Pappi!"

"My Alisa." He adds a sweet Italian accent to the s, making it sound utterly adorable. His whole expression has been ignited with life, which warms my heart. "I've been waiting for you all night. How have you been?"

"Better now that I'm here." I'm so touched by the tears forming in his eyes, I grab his hand and squeeze. This feels like a real reunion. "Sorry, I'm late. I had ah . . . a fundraiser for work."

Ashley stands back a few feet, her eyes beaming back at me. Tears are budding in her eyes, too. Most of the people in the room wear hopeful expressions, and all focus this way.

"You sound a little different." His gray eyes continue to sparkle back at me, but they don't look suspicious, rather seeped in joy.

"I'm getting over a cold." I squeeze his hand again. "Tell me, have you had any good ice cream lately?"

"Have I?" He raises both hands, exclaiming gleefully, "They have so many tubs of it here tonight, I could swim in it. Did you get any?"

"Ah, not yet." I blink, clearing my eyes. I'm not expecting to feel this emotion from something so random, but the love in Pappi's eyes radiates out.

His gaze shifts behind me, falling on Christian. "Who's this man with you?"

"Oh, that's just my boss—"

Pappi speaks over me, "—Your boyfriend?"

My gaze locks on Christian's before looking at Ashley, who jerks her head to Christian, waving him forward. "Yes, this is him. It's—"

"*Jack*," Ashley coughs out, adding an extra cough for good measure.

"Jack," I pause, afraid to offer anything more. I wasn't sure what he already knew of Jack.

"Come here, son." Pappi steels his gaze on Christian. "Let me get a good look at you."

Christian steps forward, extending a hand, which Pappi promptly takes and holds on to. "It's an honor to meet you, sir. Alisa talks about you often."

"I can't say it's nice to meet you!" Pappi angles his gaze up at Christian, his brows lowering into a scowl. "You took my granddaughter away from me and never even asked my permission."

"Woo." Christian's head startles back, but I almost bubble out a giggle. This little man is so cute, and if anyone can handle some pushback, it's Christian. "I, ah, was *scared*. Now, I'm sorry." His voice squeaks at the end, but he pushes through it. "I would love your permission now."

"I don't know if I can give it to you." Pappi shakes his head regretfully. "What do you plan to offer her?"

"Um." Christian blinks twice but holds his gaze steady, not flinching again as he goes on. "Well, I ah, have my own business, and I hope to grow it into an empire someday."

"Ah, hogwash." Pappi's lips pool in the center, as if he's getting ready to spit. "Another lady's man, ladder climber looking for a trophy wife. You want my Alisa because she's beautiful."

"No, sir. I'm not a lady's man. I hardly date at all." Christian rushes out, "And, yes, Por—, *Alisa* is stunning, but I know she's also very caring."

"Of course she's caring. I raised her. Are you a cheater?"

"No, sir. I'm very loyal. Once I commit to something, or someone, I'm all in."

My smile fades because at first, I was giggling over the pressure Pappi put on Christian, but the way Christian is being genuine with him is actually so touching, it's alarming. I cover my heart with my palm and watch.

"This feels rehearsed." Pappi turns his head away from Christian, swapping his joyful-reunion smile to one that's stone cold.

"Trust me." Christian rakes a hand through his hair, his hairline glimmering with perspiration under the fluorescent lighting. "I had no time to rehearse."

"Well, if you can pass the final question, I'll give you my blessing." Pappi rubs his wrinkled hands together, preparing to trick Christian. "Tell me, in your own words, what is love?"

Christian clears his throat. "Love is . . . love is special."

"Ah, I knew it." Pappi raises a hand, shooing him away. "You're full of bologna."

"I am not!" Christian spits back, his voice getting deeper. "I'm not a phony. Let me speak. I said it's special, but it's more than that." His gaze scans the room as if searching for a clue to tell him what to say.

I take a step forward, my heart pounding away in my chest. This is an awkward position for us both to be in. We don't even know this man. I place a hand on his arm and whisper, "It's okay, we can sneak out the fire exit."

"No." He places his hand over mine. "It's a good question. One every man should have an answer for. For me, it's like." He lets out a loud breath, and when he speaks again his voice is even lower. "W-When I was little, my mom got sick. She had asthma. Every winter, she'd get pneumonia, and her recovery was worse every year. Her doctors did what they could to prevent it, but with her weakened immune system, it was inevitable she'd spend every Christmas in bed, which broke her heart because nobody loved Christmas more than her. She always made sure to take pictures of our faces right when we opened our gifts, and she referenced them all year round." Christian's forehead beads with sweat, as if a spotlight is shining directly on it, and he shuffles his feet.

Nobody dares to make a sound, and he continues, "My dad has winters off work, since he works in construction. He had plenty of time on his hands to care for her when she fell ill. One year, she got sick right after Thanksgiving, and she couldn't get out of bed to shop for our Christmas presents, or decorate the house the way she loved it. That was the thing she enjoyed the most, and looked forward to all year. She'd look online at these décor websites and save pictures." His gaze drops to his feet, and he clears his throat again. This time, the rumbles came out hoarse.

"Dad got all of us presents, and wrapped them, writing "From Mom" on them. We all knew she didn't have anything to do with the gifts, because she was gravely ill, but Dad wanted my mom to get all of our smiles and hugs." Christian pauses again and chews on his lip. I hold my breath, as the seriousness in his tone is making my heart pound hard against my ribs.

"Dad hated decorating because it was extra work and a waste of money. That year, he bought a real Christmas tree. While she was sleeping, he set it up in her bedroom and added white lights around her bed posts. It seemed like every day he'd bring home another little elf to hide in her line of sight while she slept, or a poinsettia to set on her dresser. I even started to look forward to what new Christmas surprise we'd have each day. He used the pictures she'd saved from her websites as guidance and by the end of the season, we had a winter wonderland right in her bedroom."

I'm not fighting anymore. Tears fill my eyes, and I blink them down. From the sniffles and swiping of cheeks around the room, I know I'm not the only one. I'm completely mesmerized by what Christian is saying.

"My mom actually passed quietly in her sleep the day after Christmas. Nobody knew it was going to happen. Sometimes it still feels like a dream. In a way it was a gift. I didn't have to say a final goodbye. My last memory of her is her last Christmas night as she was watching me while I opened my expected Lego set. I looked up at my dad, eager to thank him. He had done all the work to provide for us that magical Christmas, and he definitely deserved the credit. *He wasn't even watching me.* His eyes were locked on *Mom* watching me. I was only thirteen, but I was not offended that I wasn't getting his attention. My dad couldn't take his eyes off my mom as she glowed with joy." Christian blinks as if remembering he wasn't alone. "To answer your question, I don't know much about love, but I'd never settle for anything less than that."

Tears flood down my face, and my heart pounds in my chest, melting all the previous bad thoughts I'd ever had for Christian. My dad always told me that hurt people *hurt* people. He is exactly as Arielle had said. He has a shield, and after hearing that display of his parents' love, and then losing his mom at such a young age. How could he not?

The room is dead silent, except for almost everyone sniffing behind me. "That's what I want for us," Christian tacks on with his gaze locked on me. It's so intense a sonic boom explodes in my heart as he places a hand on my hip. This is all going on in front of everyone! All these strangers don't have a clue that Christian *isn't* my real boyfriend. They assume we're dating. Christian flashes me a heart-stopping smile that is totally not a typical gaze for us. Shoot, that gaze isn't my usual gaze for anyone. My heart constricts, thumping hard against my ribcage. My chest becomes an echo chamber, expanding each thump to echo in my ears.

I'm swooning!

Flattening my palm against my chest in a feeble attempt to calm the thumping, I'm about to start fanning myself as my cheeks glow so warm I feel like I'm tanning. All eyes are on me, and everyone is waiting.

This feels like one of those cheesy movies where the couple is caught declaring their love, only we're not even a couple. I open my mouth to say something, but I'm stuck. I'm not an actress! I can't improvise this stuff. Plus, my heart is still motoring away, and it's all I can do to stare back at Christian as he fawns back at me.

"That settles it!" Pappi declares, raising his hand. My eyes pull back to him, and even Pappi has tears streaming down his face. "You have my blessing."

Christian and I crack a smile at the same time. Not a humorous one, but a secret one. I turn back to Pappi. "Thank you, Pappi. I wasn't sure when I first met him, but now I know he's one of the good ones."

"Time for you to take this girl dancing," Pappi asserts in a celebratory way. His facial expression has morphed from that sullen and dull gaze I had first seen to one that exudes life. "Cue the music. Everybody polka!"

A niggling in the back of my mind says what we're doing isn't right. Is it too much to want to add a little joy to his life? Even if it is, I'm not going to take that from him now.

I check back at Christian, hiking an inquiring brow. "Do you want to dance?"

"I wouldn't miss it," he chimes back, his eyes steel on me, as if I'm his whole world. He's clearly still acting like my boyfriend for Pappi's sake.

I swallow as a lump buds in my throat, but it's nothing I can't ignore. What are we getting into? I don't have time to ponder as a polka blasts through the ceiling speakers. Christian wraps an arm around my shoulders and whisks me to the dance floor. The cozy little floor fills with couples who are mostly at least double, if not triple, our age. We follow their lead, holding our hands, extending them out. "Ah, problem." I'm smiling because the music has already lightened the somber mood of the room. "I have no idea what a polka is."

"It's basically a hopping two-step. I go to the left, it's your right." Christian starts slow, as he waits for me to catch on.

"And you know this how?" I hop twice and stop, forgetting to come back on the return, but Christian adjusts, waiting for me.

"Lots of Saturday nights with my grandma." He lifts his arm above his head, pulling me. "Let me guide you."

Chuckling, I traipse over his feet as I complete what I think is supposed to be a twirl. "You better not dip me," I joke. "Anything that takes me off both feet will cause you great suffering."

"Trust me, after the fall down the subway, I've been babying my back all week." He pulls my arms up, and I spin again. We repeat this pattern until the music is over, with me stomping on at least one of his feet at least every other spin.

"Sorry." I giggle through a wince as the music transitions to another song, and we break apart, heading off the dance floor. "I should have warned you that I don't polka."

"Clearly, you should have disclosed that on your job application."

Enjoying the sarcasm, I run my mouth. "I'm sorry to say, but I had every intention of deceiving you."

"I knew it all along." Playfully pointing an accusing finger at me, his voice turns serious. "What else have you been deceiving me about?"

"Oh." I rack my brain, digging for something witty, as I recall our rough start. Not wanting to lose my comedic timing, I rush to banter back, "Maybe I was only pretending to hate you, because I actually like you."

What did I just spew out!

Halting my feet, my eyes swell as my words ring back through my ears. My insides ice over, and I beg my mouth to take back my words—or spout off something funny—but nothing comes up my vocal cords.

It was a joke! I beg my mouth to say, but it won't listen.

In a rush to be funny, I didn't think how that would sound. Christian tilts his head toward me with an intense gaze that *melts my feet to the floor!* It's that look couples have at the moment everything changes, and I feel it reverberate all the way to my toes.

Bringing his chin down, he hovers his gaze intensely on mine. "Portia, did you mean that?"

"No," I spit out, tacking on, "Yes. I mean, maybe. Do you?"

He does not take his eyes off me.

All the love songs that have ever been sung about this moment seem to play in my head, and they've all been rewritten just for us. For the second time tonight my heart motors at top speed, and it's all I can do not to fall over dead.

He lowers his chin, aligning his face with mine, and as he starts to bring his lips down, a giant, extra pokey elbow from a child running behind me jabs me in my side. I stumble and blurt, "Ouch!"

Rubbing my side, I take a deep breath and prepare to return my gaze to Christian. Christian's smirking now. The moment clearly passed, but I hold my breath anyway.

Things are about to change.

TWENTY-FOUR

Christian

"That turned out to be a fun evening." I chuckle as I pull my car slowly into her parking lot and creep to a stop. "And again, we didn't kill each other."

"We've both gone crazy." Her eyes sparkle but neither of us move to exit the vehicle. We've been sharing these lingering moments all night.

She doesn't move.

I don't move.

We stare at each other as if meeting each other for the first time, yet it feels so familiar.

Familiar *and* exciting.

More exciting than familiar.

There's an airy feeling in my chest, making me lighter, and I feel as if I could laugh myself silly for days.

If anyone had asked me even two days ago if I would ever be able to stand Portia, I would have had a hard time believing it is possible. Now, I can't take my eyes off of her. She is stunning. Which I had always known...even though I would never admit it. She didn't have the type of beauty you see in magazines: nothing is overly made up about her, unlike all the women I saw tonight at the fundraiser. She's a true natural beauty, exactly like my mother had been.

Only in a slightly different font.

"Do you need me to walk you up the stairs?" I know the answer is no but I can't say goodnight. I also don't want to come off as some creep who is only walking her upstairs to try to get an invitation inside her apartment. That's not the kind of guy I am.

"Well, the elevator's still broken, and it's late." Her voice drops to a whisper at the end, and I barely hear her pronounce the T. Her eyes round even more, pulling me into her endless spirals of beryl-blue hues. "I'm sure you're tired."

It sounds like a goodbye, but she doesn't even move her pinky to graze the door handle. Once again, we gaze at each other, frozen. Don't get me wrong, I don't mind it. I feel so alive, and I don't ever want this feeling to end. I'm hesitating because I don't want to push anything. "Thanks for ah, coming out tonight."

"You're welcome." Her upper teeth clamp down on her lower lip, flushing the pink tissue into white. My heart jerks out a massive flutter as if it's having a seizure.

She is clearly waiting for me to kiss her!

As much as I want to, it doesn't feel right.

I'm her boss.

We work together.

We don't date.

We clearly don't kiss.

The thing is . . . I want to kiss her.

We had an amazing time tonight.

But I'm not the guy who goes around kissing girls because we had one night of fun. When I fall, I plummet heart first. I'm not sure what this flirtation even is. Are we riding on the coattails of Pappi's party where we pretended to like each other? I don't want to suffer in the long run for this. I break our gaze, rake my fingers through my hair, and toss a look forward over the steering wheel. "I'll see ya tomorrow at work, right?"

She startles, sitting up straighter. "Yeah, I come in at three to close."

"I'll be opening for El if she's not feeling better."

"I'll see you then." She pauses, sways forward as if testing a leanin, but I keep my eyes fixed ahead.

"Bye." My word is extra choppy, and I don't steal even a tiny glance as she climbs out of the car. I'm such a jerk to not walk her to her door. The thing is, I can't ward off another one of those moments while standing next to her. I open my window, letting in cold air, and inhale it deeply.

I should be better in the morning. This is a weird fluke. We clearly got caught up in the dancing and acting like a couple stuff. I wait in the car until she's safely in the building. Then I wait longer—nine more minutes to be exact—until I see a light flash on in her apartment window. No, that's not creepy at all. It's one hundred percent gentleman. Now that I know she's safe, I can go home.

As I drive, my mind wanders to Pappi. The whole skit we had pulled on him had started off as a friendly gesture we didn't think would last more than a minute or two. We ended up spending the evening joking, eating and laughing with his family, as if we were family. Everyone in that room was supporting him in his final days, and I don't regret what we did for him. Ashley had said privately he'd spent the last year in a bit of a homesick stupor, since he couldn't understand why his Alisa didn't call. Maybe someday God will punish us for what we did tonight. I can't help that at this moment I am honored to have met him. He will leave a lasting impression on me.

I shake my head as I turn the corner, returning to my hotel. "Life's so short. Who's to say you're owed any time?"

Thinking of my own grandma and how she ignored my call, a sour taste coats in my throat. We used to be so close. I'd assumed she'd eventually come around to understanding why I didn't want to run a construction company. It seems silly now. In the big picture, does the job you have really matter?

I park in my hotel parking lot, but don't shut off my car right away. Instead, I pull out my phone and construct the perfect text for my grandma. One to explain to her everything I was feeling and everything I had felt all these weeks we weren't talking. This isn't about me not having money to pay my loan. I need her to know how much I miss her. I type and delete so many words because I have so much to say to her. In the end, after nearly thirty minutes of analyzing every word combo, I settle on the perfect text.

Me: I love you, Grandma.

I reread it, a reminiscent grin lacing my lips as I press send. I don't stow my phone away just yet. I had a hunch about something. I quickly construct another text.

Me: Portia, thank you for tonight.

I press send as fast as I can before losing my nerve and go inside.

TWENTY-FIVE
Portia

"Dad?" I answer my phone before my eyes are even open the following morning.

"Did Oliver catch anything this morning?"

"What?" Pressing on my forehead, I force my mind to focus on the present. "What time is it?"

"Almost noon."

"No way." I pull myself to a seated position and squint at my alarm clock—11:47. Yep, almost noon. I can't believe I slept that long. I don't remember waking up once or even dreaming. It was the most restful sleep I'd had in a while. "Ah, I'm still in bed. I overslept."

"Are you feeling okay?"

"I think so." Curious myself, I swipe my forehead with the back of my hand and run my hand down my cheek.

Nothing feels warm. "I was out late last night at a fundraiser thing for work." Scooting to the edge of the bed, I slip my feet into my slippers and stand. "Are you heading to Home Hardware?"

"No, not today since it's New Year's Eve. I want to invite you over for a bowl of my famous chili later. We could watch the ball drop on TV."

"Well, you do have the best chili, but I close tonight. It will be after eight by the time I get everything cleaned up." Rubbing my chin, I did the time math. "Can I call you when I'm almost done with my shift? Depending on how busy we are, I may be too tired to come over."

"I'll keep it in the crockpot, and it will be ready whenever."

"Sounds good." Mr. Noodles flies out from under the sink, where apparently he'd been sleeping. He loves resting in there, especially when it's extra warm inside, and I haven't been leaving the window cracked anymore. His eyes are on me as he slinks next to his bowl and nudges it forward. "I better go, Dad. Someone needs breakfast."

When I end my call, a text message flashes on my screen.

Christian: Portia, Thank you for tonight.

A zap slams into my gut, bringing back all the tingles from last night, and I'm instantly giddy inside. I had vowed to try to be friends with him. What I never expected was to see him so vulnerable. When he explained what love was to him, I literally melted like lava in an active volcano. I'd never heard any man speak about something so swoony in my life.

Everything feels different after last night. Christian isn't that stone-faced person he'd been. Truthfully, he felt different for the last couple of days. But this was even more different, different. It's more than trying to be friends. Like when I look at him, my breath gets trapped in my lungs.

I can't even remember what it was like not to hate him anymore.

I get to see him in a few hours, but I still need to walk Oliver. I rise to my feet and hurry to the cupboard, grabbing Mr. Noodles' sack of dry food. It's not the stuff he wants. I've been out of canned food for a couple of days as my temporary lack of employment had put a halt to my shopping. I'll have to stop at the store on my way home from work or he'll start to get moody.

"Alright, Mr. Noodles," I sing out, as I roll up the top of his food bag, sealing off the air. "You are all set. Now I need to get some more recruits."

As if it has ears, my phone bleeps. It's my app, sending me messages. I can't keep up. I've been casually messaging a few guys, most of them are boring. When I open my app, I'm greeted with a "Level Up" message, stating I'm eligible to share my name with this one guy.

He's the one who makes me smile with his sarcasm, and he's spent the last two days trying to get me to type the letter Y. We haven't chatted a ton. In a way, that makes me like him more. Like he has a life outside of cruising for hotties online. I clamp down on my lips and pause. I knew this request was coming. I'm the one who designed the app, but was I ready to tell someone online my name?

But what could it hurt? Just a first name.

Then we can chat for another week before I am forced to decide if I want to share a pic. Before I overthink it, I accept the request, type in my name and press send. He'll also have to accept the request before I can hear back. My stomach twists thinking about it.

I breathe out a cleansing breath, and throw my coat on, while slipping my feet into my sneakers. I've got a dog to walk, and recruits to find.

I can't say I've ever been excited to work on New Year's Eve before. Other years, it felt like a bad omen. Since I don't have exciting plans—other than eating chili with my parents—I look forward to getting out of the house.

Who am I kidding?

My blood is ripping through my veins with adrenaline because I can't stop thinking about Christian. Had I imagined all that chemistry last night? I'm dying to see if he'd act any differently today. What if, by some amazing miracle, we end up working so super late, and one thing *leads to another and we share a midnight kiss?*

I blush so hard my toenails rouge.

I pace my tiny apartment, smoothing my hair several times as Mr. Noodles' head swings back and forth as if he is watching a giant pendulum. What will I say to Christian? Do I pretend everything's professional? Well, everything technically is still professional on the outside.

Inside, my heart won't stop belting out rapid beats. I tilt my head to the side, remembering how he rakes his hand through his hair when nervous. He has great hair. And he takes care of his sister. That feels honorable. And we both love coffee. Still, who doesn't?

That one doesn't count.

He did save my life when I was choking.

Gotta give him that much.

Yep, that solves it.

Saving my life means he's a keeper.

I am clearly smitten.

I don't want to wait another minute to see him, and I rush out of the door. The air is brisk, but the sun is shining exceptionally brightly. The kind of brightness you see in all your best memories.

Strolling through the crowds of people on the sidewalk, I can't break the smile on my face, and my toes curl. I make it to work in record time, and my phone bleeps. It's my app, but I ignore it. Inhaling a final breath of fresh air, I open the door and immediately search for Christian. My heart stops pumping without notice, and I freeze.

He's standing by the window. As his gaze meets mine, I can't pretend I don't feel chemistry. "Hey." I throw my hand up in a soft wave. "How are you?"

"So much is going on right now." He tilts his head to the side, as if he's weighing a decision. "So much is happening, and the room is spinning."

"What's wrong?"

"Well, two things. First." He flashes his phone at me with an unreadable text message on the screen. "I have been trying to reach my grandmother for a few days without hearing anything back. I thought she was ignoring me. I finally got a reply from my dad on her behalf. She's not doing well."

"Oh." My heart immediately aches for him, and I so badly want to give him a hug, but instead I wring my hands together. "I'm sorry."

"El is feeling mostly better, and we're planning to go see her. The only flights available are tomorrow night. We don't want to wait that long and are considering driving." Flecks of sorrow flash in his eyes. "I just need someone to cover the store."

"I can do it." I drop my purse on the nearby table, as it suddenly feels heavy.

"We shouldn't be gone long, and you can close early when it's slow."

"It's no problem." I wave my hand dismissively. "My dad can always stop by and give me a break. Maybe Jade can cover a shift or two. I don't think she's found work since you fired her. I'm guessing you won't care."

"No, I don't mind, and I would actually love that because I don't want you to overextend yourself."

I roll my lips in, holding them in pause, feeling how heavy this conversation is. "You don't have to worry about a thing. I ran this place by myself before you got here. Go now if you need to."

"Thanks." He runs his fingers through his hair, not doing anything to smooth it down as it becomes more disheveled. "I, ah, this is weird." He balls his hand into a fist, holding it near his core. "I know this is not the right time, but I don't know when I'll be back, but something just happened."

"What?" My heart's skipping along, waiting for the punchline.

He doesn't speak. Instead, he turns back to his phone, clicks on something and flashes it back at me. I squint, ready for another cryptic message from his grandma, but it's something I recognize.

My eyes spring open, and I literally scream. "What!"

It's my website.

My dating website on his phone, and a Match Name Reveal is on his phone:

Portia Grant from Long Island.

What?

I yank my phone out from my pocket. My fingers flutter as I trace my password, and sure enough on my phone, there's a Match Name Reveal:

Christian Hanson from Long Island.

I'm dead. How did that happen?

"I, ah," he stutters while staring down on my phone. "El found a free match card outside and made me use it."

"It's my website," I blurt out. "I own it, and I, ah, dropped all those cards."

"Matchmaking?" He plants his feet an arm's reach away from me. Not my arm. My arms are quite petite, but his arms. His arms are long and muscular, and all of the sudden I can't stop looking at them.

"Yeah, it's a small, inclusive matchmaking app I run with my dad. It was initially my idea. He helped me research and paid to have it developed. It's one of the most fine-tuned matching algorithms in existence."

"So, this is real?" He motions back to his phone, my name still flashing in the middle.

"I think so." I feel the smile he gives me all the way to my toes. Relieved we are on the same page, I wish I could take another step closer, but now isn't the time. I can't leave him hanging, but what do I say? I'm stunned, and shocked, and stunned again. "Ah, I'm so glad you said something, because I hadn't checked my phone yet. That might have been weird if we'd never brought it up."

"Not going to be weird at all." He chuckles, dropping his hand back to his side as his face lights up in a glowing rouge. "I mean, I'm always a little weird, but I can't change that. I've honestly tried."

"Good, because I don't want things to be *weird*."

"So right. It's not going to be *weird*." He flashes a glance at his wristwatch and then back at me. "I hate to leave like this."

"Go." I wave him out the door. "I'm fine."

His feet cement to the floor, and he gives me that look again. The one that borders between flirting and pining, and I do everything possible to stay in control of my legs. All I want to do is lean in for a kiss. Thankfully, he steels his gaze to the exit. "I'll text you when I get there."

Ah, yes! I scream in my head, while excitement pulses through my veins and I force myself to remain calm, despite my insides scrambling in a tangled knot. "Sure, I'd like that." I hold my hand up, as he pivots and heads out the door. "Drive safe."

My heart instantly plummets. I'm spending New Year's Eve alone, working. It has such a different ring to it after planning to spend the shift with Christian. I pick up my phone to text.

Me: Dad, chili sounds great. I'll be over to watch the ball.

Sighing, I drag my feet toward the coffee bar and grab my French press. Might as well have some coffee because it's going to be a long, boring, and lonely night.

I arrive at my parents' house with a grocery sack of cat food I grabbed on the way over. Without knocking, I let myself into their townhouse. "I'm here."

Slipping off my shoes, I flex my feet as they start to relax after standing on them all day. After setting my sack by the entrance, I meander into the kitchen, where Dad sits at the table with his tablet. Motor noises waft from the screen.

"Happy New Year, Dad." I plop into the chair next to him. "Where's Mom?"

"Happy New Year to you." He doesn't take his eyes off his race. I peek over his shoulder. He's driving a red car, and it has number one for first place on the leaderboard on top of his screen. "She's taking a bath. She put her curlers in, so it might be a while."

I smile at how such a mundane detail of putting curlers in serves as a flag to Dad, letting him know she needs more time. Sinking lower into the chair, I rest my elbow on the table and plop my chin into my palm.

"What's his name?" Dad asks without taking his eyes from his tablet.

I tsk. "There's nobody—"

Dad hikes a brow, and that's all it takes to make me cave. "It's my boss, Christian. I thought he was a jerk, but something happened yesterday." My words spew out, like I'm that crazy lady who over shares at a bar. Only I'm not at a bar, I'm with my dad. He's the one person I trust more than anything, so I keep talking. "We went to this fundraiser thing for work, and it ended up being a weird night, but it was sort of the best night. We were supposed to work together today, but he left town for a family emergency. I'm bummed because I wanted to see him, but it's selfish since he's having family issues."

Dad lays his tablet on the table without pausing his race. Cars fly by him, and his number slips to 2, 3, 4, 5. He's losing, or as he prefers to call it, "He's getting smoked." He doesn't take a second look back when he gets up. "What are you doing?" I ask.

"Getting pie." He opens the fridge, his head disappearing inside, and I hear rummaging.

"I thought you had chili."

He reappears with a pan of half-eaten blueberry pie, grabs two forks from the sink drying rack, and plops it on the table in front of me. "Eat." He hands me a fork, as if it's a weapon that can tackle my heartsickness.

Dad takes his fork and scrapes off the edge of the pie. I peel away at the opposite end. After several bites of silence, oddly, I'm feeling better. Dad says, "Did you know that desserts is stressed spelled backwards?"

"You always know the best conspiracies?" I lick the blueberry sauce from the handle of my fork, as this is so much messier than it should be.

"Who said anything about conspiracies." He lays down his fork. "That's a fact."

My dad had an uncanny way of saying all the right things by saying nothing at all and just eating pie. I still want his advice, though. Admitting I have a crush is a big step. I've been running from love for a long time. Not that this is love but I avoid even considering dating. "What do you think I should do, Dad?"

He scratches his cheek while studying my face. "You say this boy's coming back after his emergency?"

"Yeah, his business is here. So, he has to come back."

"You call that boy and tell him that your dad knows his way around a hardware store. If I need to make a body disappear, I won't have any problem doing it."

"Dad," I rush to interrupt him. "You don't have to worry about that."

"I don't have to worry if you do what I say." He raises two fingers, making a V and points to his eyes. "I'll watch him like a dad so you don't have to worry about a thing."

"I'm done talking about this, because you're starting to get weird." I push my chair back and crane my neck to peer down the hall. "It is getting late. Should I go say hi to mom? I don't know if I want to stay until midnight. I might try to catch the last train to Forest Hills."

"Nah, let her rest. She puts up with me all day." His grin sprouts slowly and grows until it fills his whole face. Their relationship always feels cute to me. It's not one from the fairytales, but there's a steadiness, and companionship that's lasted decades.

"Okay." I move toward the door. "I have canned food for Mr. Noodles. I'd better get home before he jumps out the window again."

"Sounds good. Happy New Year." He picks up his tablet, resuming his racing game as if I'd already left.

"Yeah, Happy New Year." I jerk my thumb toward the counter. "Can I grab some chili to go? I never had dinner."

"I don't have any chili." He pulls the tablet closer to his face as he steers his car around the track.

I blink, dumbfounded. "You asked me to come over for chili."

"That's what I said to get you to come over here to tell me about this boy."

My mouth falls open. "How did you—"

He taps rapidly on his tablet with his gaze down. "I have my ways."

"I didn't know there was a boy until now." Placing a hand on my hip, recalling what I'd said that would have tipped him off, but there was nothing. "How could you know?"

"I could hear it in your voice this morning when I called. You were frazzled—"

"Dad," I cut him off, but he stops me by standing and dropping his tablet back to the table. "It's okay, honey. This is exactly what you need." Extending his arms out, he invites me for a hug.

I smash my lips together, holding in all my quivers, and walk forward. It's an embrace that always comforts me, even when I'm being stubborn. I'm smiling again by the time I pull back. "Okay." I point down the hall. "Tell Mom Happy New Year. Wait a second." I tap my finger to my chin. "Is Mom even in the tub?"

"Nope. Went to bed two hours ago. That's what I said to get you to stay. If you knew she was in bed, you'd have felt guilty for staying." He winks at me, nodding toward the door. "Better get home."

"Deal." I slip on my shoes while speaking over my shoulder. "I'm working extra for a while, so I won't have time for Home Hardware for a few days. I'll call you as soon as I have a break."

"It's okay." Dad shakes his head. "I don't want to go to Home Hardware. I'm sick of that place."

"What are you talking about?" I blink, rewinding his words. "You love going there."

"Nah, reminds me of work. I only went there to find you a man, but it seems you might have actually found one. So, no, I don't need to go."

"You're making this up."

"Believe what you want." He walks to the front window, pulls back the curtain, and takes a protective stance.

"Are you going to watch me walk down the street?" I retrieve my grocery sack and open the door, already knowing the answer to my question.

"Yep, and text me when you get home."

"Love you, Dad."

"Love you, too."

Now that I know Mom is sleeping, I close the door as softly as I can. My dad is a turkey. There's no way he can be telling the truth. We've gone to Home Hardware together for a year. He wouldn't have done it if he hated it. Plus, he hasn't even met Christian.

There's no way he would know.

He can't know.

I shake my head, heading down the street at a brisk walking pace.

Could he know? Wait. What's there to know?

Now I want to know.

TWENTY-SIX

Christian

I tap lightly on my grandmother's bedroom door, not moving even a toe inside. The pit of my stomach feels heavy and sour as dread consumes me. "Grandma," I whisper. "You awake?"

"Christian, is that you?" Her voice sounds more tired than usual, but not weak.

"Yeah." Accepting that as an invitation, I walk forward until she can see me. She looks like her same old self, with straight dark hair ratted in the back from laying down. Her skin is relatively warm toned for someone who is ill. Wheel of Fortune plays on the wall TV, and she has a tray with several glasses of fluids next to her. If I didn't know better, I would say it was an ordinary day for her. But I do know better, and I step forward respectfully. "How are you?"

"Well, I've heard it might be my time to go, but I'm not going to listen to that." She looks at me straight, her eyelids fluttering closed before she pulls them open again. "Plus, you and I have some business to talk about."

I lower my eyes to the floor. The heaviness consumes me. "Grandma, you don't have to talk about anything."

"Nope." She adjusts the linen blanket, pulling it tighter around her. "I've been unfair to you. We both know that."

As much as I want to agree with her, I don't. I also want to ask what made her change her mind, but it didn't matter now. "It's all right."

"Well, here's the deal." Her tone sounds a tad exploratory, as if she's not quite sure what the deal actually is. "I always knew you weren't right for Total Trucks."

"How so?"

"You're the only boy I'd ever seen beg for a seatbelt when given the chance to drive a dump truck." Her lips pull into a sweet grin, but her eyelids droop so low, I can barely see her pupils. "I didn't think it was fair that your mom got sick. I had made up my mind that all the rest of my dreams would come true if I held on to them. I was being stubborn, but I have never been prouder of you. You followed your own path despite the pressure I put on you. You are always my sweet Christian."

A dam of tears wells in my eyes. My mom used to call me her sweet Christian. I hadn't heard that in years. The nickname echoes in my heart, melting the barrier I'd built up to keep it from being hurt. An instant release of the pressure I'd felt for years opens my chest, and I'm able to breathe so much deeper. I don't fight the release, as I would have done in the past. I allow my stress to erase with each new breath, the knots untangling even more. "Thank you."

Her eyes seal all the way tight. "Your mom would have been so proud of you, too."

I breathe into that compliment as it hits my gut like a stone. It isn't something I'd ever let myself consider. I flash my gaze to heaven. Not in the annoying way I usually roll my eyes, but instead I check for signs of Mom. Despite the many years of searching, I've never gotten a clear sign. "I hope so," I murmur while I silently pray it's loud enough for her to hear.

A pleasant grin sweeps over her lips as her chest rises further now, and settles into deep, restful breaths. I tiptoe to the edge of the bed, drop a kiss on her cheek, and turn to leave.

In the hallway, I catch the end of El's ponytail sneaking out the back door, and I whisper-holler her way. "Hey, where are you going?" She doesn't hear me as the door latches behind her.

I approach the door, and my gaze follows her to a truck parked a couple of houses down the street. I don't recognize it, but that doesn't surprise me. She climbs into the cab, and two seconds later they are driving down the road.

"What are you up to, El?" I ask out loud, knowing full well this has to do with the mystery dude she's been wallowing about. Maybe they can straighten things out? Maybe that would mean she couldn't stay in New York? There's an awful lot of maybes. I haven't even gotten to the one that's strongest in the back of my mind. Maybe I should text Portia?

I walk back down the hall to the living room and drop onto the couch. It's hours past dark, after an exhaustingly long day. This is as good a place as any to sleep, and I stretch my legs out while pulling a throw blanket over me. I unlock my phone, and it flashes 12:01. I smile as I type a text.

Me: Happy New Year.

Flicking my thumb off the edge of my phone, I weigh the decision of whether to send it so late. I told Portia I'd text. She won't expect something this late. I don't want to wake her since she has to get up at five to work. But what if she's awake? What if she went out? We never talked about our plans for the holiday. What if she met some dude on her website, and they're toasting right now? I tug my fingers through my front spike and wince. I'm making myself go crazy. It's just a text.

I press send, staring at my phone, holding my breath as it gets marked "Read." Then, the screen changes to texting dots, and my heart motors rapidly.

Portia: Happy New Year to you, too!

"Phew." I blew out a breath. Not sure why this is so hard. Oh wait, she is typing more. I suck in a hard breath and wait.

Portia: Did you make it to Massachusetts okay?

Me: Yeah, we got in about an hour ago. Grandma's resting. El snuck out the backdoor to meet some hick in a truck, and I'm getting ready to go to sleep.

Portia: Was it blue and white?

Squinting as if it can help me see into my memory better, I think back.

Me: Yeah, I think so. Why?

Portia: That's Tom's.

Me: Who's Tom?

I type rapidly now, shooting off a stream of steady texts.

Me: How do you know about Tom?

Me: Do you know where they went?

Portia: They dated, but she suspected he might be married because all their dates were always secret.

Me: Yeah, why was he hiding on the street?

Portia: I mean, your guess is as good as mine.

Me: He better not play her or he's going to get it.

Portia: Speaking of such things, my dad told me to tell you he knows his way around a hardware store and he's an expert at disposing of dead bodies.

I chuckle. Of course she can't be serious.

Me: Why were you talking to your dad about me?

Portia: ?

Me: What does ? mean?

Portia: I might have said we went to a fundraiser last night.

Me: Is that all?

Portia: You tell me. Is that all?

Me: It didn't feel like it.

Me: I wish I could see you tonight.

Portia: Yeah, me too.

Me: I'd better let you sleep since you have to run my store for me.

Portia: K.

Me: Are you tired?

Portia: Maybe

Me: What are you thinking about?

Portia: You.

An arrow splices through my heart, and I drop my phone to rest on my chest. Something about late night texting doesn't feel real. Is she playing with me? I wish I could see her expression. I grapple for my phone and reply before she thinks I ghosted her.

Me: Good.

Me: I'm thinking about you, too.

Me: But you need to go to sleep.

Portia: Night.

Me: Night.

I set my phone down, keeping the text open, rereading the part where she says she's thinking about me over and over. Smiling so big, like I haven't done in years. There's not a doubt I care about this girl. Man, I wish I would have kissed her when I had the chance.

If I get a chance again, I won't hold back.

TWENTY-SEVEN

I lean over the counter at the Coffee Loft as my phone
lights up.

Christian: How's the store?

Me: A little rush this morning. Now it's slow.

Biting my lip, I press send and wait. It's only a mere
moment later, and my screen lights up again.

Christian: Does ur boss know you text at work?

My smile is instant.

**Me: He does now. But I don't think it will matter.
He's already fired me once. Then he found out he
can't live without me, and begged me to come back.**

Christian: He sounds like a jerk.

Me: I used to think so.

Hovering my thumb over my phone, I figure now is as good of a time as any to be honest.

Me: Now, I think I might like him a little.

Christian: So, you forgave him for firing you?

Me: I think so.

Christian: That's good.

Me: How's your grandma?

I press send, and then scan the store to make sure none of the remaining customers need anything. Everybody looks fine. I return my gaze to my phone as another text comes in.

Christian: Waking for shorter periods.

Me: I'm sorry to hear that. R U OK?

Christian: Yeah, we had a nice chat right when I got here. That helps.

Me: Well, if it helps, everything is fine here. Take as much time as you need.

Me: Is it weird that we are texting, and we barely know each other?

Christian: No, because I know a lot about you.

Me: Oh really?

**Christian: Yeah, I know you steal Oreos, have an awesome boss, live in a Rapunzel tower, have a cat with a murderous spirit. You are daddy's princess, you can't dance, and have an awful preference for French press coffee. You have a handsome boss, and

stunning blue eyes, and did I mention your boss is a stud?

I giggle as I read through his description of me, and my heart nearly skips a beat each time he mentions how cool he is.

Me: Wow. You know a lot.

Christian: What do you know about me?

Me: I know you

My thumb slips and I accidentally press send when I meant to delete it.

Christian: You know me what?

Me: Never mind.

Christian: No, tell me.

Me: I know you love your sister, your grandma, and your business. I know you loved your mom. I know your definition of love, and I love it.

Christian: You know you're at work and have been texting for twenty minutes. Your boss is going to be so mad at you.

Chuckling, my mind flashes to when Christian was furious with me for standing outside his store. I swore I saw steam come out of his ears. I can't believe we are even talking, but somehow it worked out.

Me: I don't care.

Christian: That's a bold statement.

Me: Something tells me he'd approve.

Christian: I better let you go, or he's going to fire you again.

Me: Ok. 1 more question.

Christian: No, you can't have a raise.

Me: Really?! You wouldn't give me a raise after seeing how amazing I am?

Christian: Okay, change that. I'll adjust your pay for the next check.

Me: Mean that?

Christian: I do. I appreciate you putting up with me.

Me: Are you trying to buy my affection?

Christian: No, but would it work?

Me: No.

Christian: Clock's ticking and boss man is going to be livid. What's your question?

Me: Ah, a customer just walked in. Text me later. I'll see if you're worthy of it.

I rest my phone on the counter and stare out into the empty Coffee Loft lobby. Nobody is here. I didn't even accidentally hear something that sounded like a customer. I made that last part up when I lost my nerve.

And it's good to play a little hard to get.

TWENTY-EIGHT
Christian

Finally lifting myself out of Grandma's bedroom armchair, where I had sat with her all night, I stretch with my arms high over my head. Since I don't have to work, I volunteered for the overnight shift. Now it's after seven in the morning, and the sun is fully up.

"How is she?" El peeks her head into the open door. Grandma refuses to go to the hospital, and we are all rotating shifts, not leaving her alone. It's hard to believe she's so ill, as she appears peaceful. "She's resting. Hasn't complained, or made a peep."

"Well, I'll be here all day. Why don't you get some sleep?" She pads into the room and sinks down into the armchair. "You don't want to get run down."

"I'll rest later. I'm going for a quick walk to loosen up. I'm super stiff. Is there anything you need from the store?"

"No, I'm okay, and Dad will be here in an hour or so." She jerks her head forcefully toward the door now, shooing me away. "I promise. I'll call if anything changes, but you need to take a break. You look like a zombie."

"Grandma," I whisper, before I lean in and drop a kiss on her cheek. "I love you." Her eyelashes flutter but don't open, and I know she feels me here.

I back out of the room, heading outside, and allow my breaths to deepen in the fresh air. Fresh frost has blanketed the city, making the trees sparkle in the early light. With no plan, I walk toward downtown, where a small diner used to be. I'm not hungry, but coffee sounds good. It's not Coffee Loft coffee, but it'll work. Speaking of Coffee Loft, I pull out my phone to check in.

Me: Are you at work?

Portia: Depends. Are you asking as my boss, or as that guy I've been texting?

I've heard the expression that your heart can skip a beat, but I always assumed it was an expression. Now I know that to be the truth. My heart literally skips a beat.

Me: I'll go with option B.

Portia: Oh, that's not an option right now because I'm at work.

Me: OK. As your boss, how is work?

Portia: Everything is fine.

Me: I'll take my question now please?

Portia: What question?

Me: Don't do that.

I flash my gaze to the sky. This woman really does know how to drive me crazy.

Portia: Do what?

Me: Pretend you don't know what I'm talking about. I have a whole string of text messages that leaves a solid paper trail clearly showing you have a question to ask me.

Portia: Oh, that question. How's the weather there?

Me: It's about to get crazy if someone doesn't tell me what they are up to.

Portia: Who said I was up to anything?

Me: You seriously don't have a question for me?

I pause on the corner and wait for the crossing sign to change to 'walk.' People are out, and the city Christmas tree is still up in the town square. All that time in Grandma's house had left me feeling in a trance, like nothing was real anymore. It's weird to think how life goes on, despite what anybody's going through. I cross the street and then check my phone.

Portia: Not right now.

Me: What if I guess?

Portia: You can try.

Me: Okay, you were going to ask me if I like long walks on the beach?

Portia: No.

Me: Oh, well, the answer is yes.

Portia. Ok

Me: Do you like long walks on the beach?

Portia: I don't really think I've ever taken a long walk on the beach. Just a short one across it. Who do you take long walks on the beach with?

Me: Nobody.

Portia: You walk by yourself?

Me: Sometimes when I'm back here, I like to walk along the harbor.

Portia: Interesting.

Me: Next guess. Were you going to ask me what my hobbies are?

Portia: No. You seem like a pretty boring guy who doesn't have a life outside of work.

Me: That's almost right. Except, I do have some hobbies. I'll list them in alphabetical order so you can jot them down. Expert at Uno, the card game, not counting. Reading. Amateur at playing guitar (five-string bass), and dancing the polka with you.

I walk right to the center of Townsquare and pause at the city gazebo, taking a seat on the steps. It's chilly out, but the fresh air feels so good, and I'm able to breathe so much more deeply than I have in weeks, and it's invigorating.

Portia: That's not in alphabetical order.

Me: Yeah, I saved the best for last.

Portia: I hate to break it to you, but I don't think I'll ever dance the polka again.

Me: You really shouldn't. You were terrible.

Me: Next question. Were you going to ask me what my favorite childhood memory is?

Portia: Nope, that wasn't even on my radar, but why don't you go ahead and tell.

Me: Don't mind if I do. You know how Christmas mornings were a big deal at my house, right?

Portia: Yeah

Me: That.

Portia: What about that?

Me: All of that. All of the mornings. Can't pick one.

Me: Same question to you.

Portia: Well, I played a lot of Barbies when I was little, so anytime Barbie got married was fun, which was like every other day. I don't know if I can pick just one.

Me: Right, those memories are clearly overshadowed by that stupendous day you first met me.

Chuckling, I consider laying off the silly bragging, but I'm waiting to see if I can get her to agree to anything. Just once I want to hear her say she likes me.

Portia. You seem fairly confident.

Me: Oh, were you going to ask me about my ideal date night?

Portia: No. I wasn't going to ask you that.

Me: I wasn't going to answer you about that.

Me: Okay, you want to know my favorite movie? I'll tell you. The Sandlot.

Portia: I love that movie too!

Me: I have fond memories of it. What's yours?

Portia: It's hard to pick just one.

Me: Give me five.

Portia: I'll say I love romcom, and all those cheesy Christmas movies.

Me: Gah! I just went blind.

Portia: How's your grandma?

Me: Resting. Peaceful. El is with her.

Portia: That's good.

Me: Can I have my question now?

Portia: Ask me tomorrow. I'm too tired now.

Me: Tomorrow is Wednesday.

Portia: Oops. Coffee Loft is on fire. Gotta go!

Chuckling, I picture Portia's face when we locked gazes at the fundraiser. A lot has changed since that night. Clearly our opinions of each other have improved. It's weird how we didn't know it then, but a spry old man named Pappi was exactly what we both needed to get past our giant egos. We really aren't that different when it comes to our stubbornness.

I can't wait to see her again. Maybe it's all in my head, but she's texting like she likes me, too.

Sighing, I stand back up and head toward the diner.

Now, if only I can get her to admit she likes me.

TWENTY-NINE

Portia

Three days have passed since I've heard from Christian, and it feels much longer. It's funny how you think you know what you want in life, and then something simple like someone coming into your life changes everything. I haven't been obsessing over my female to male ratio on my website at all the last few days. Sure, I hand out QR codes, but then I leave it up to fate. So far, the website hasn't crashed. I take that as a good sign. It actually feels healthy for me to take a small step back from my website now. I check it but only once a day, as opposed to at least once every hour.

I'm completely whipped when I crawl into bed. I've been hoping Christian texts me, harassing me to tell him my question. I toy with the idea of texting him with a random clue to my question, but since he is the one spending time with family, I keep my space.

I tap my phone, not engaging any letters to actually type. It's too early in this situationaship for me to justify bothering him at his grandma's, but I can't help but wish my phone would light up with a text. I have no idea how long I stare at my phone but without noticing, I nod off.

Sometime in the early morning, I wake up to my phone chiming.

Christian: I'm headed out for a morning walk. Want to talk with me?

Me: Ok.

Christian: Tell me your ideal match.

Me: Excuse me?

Christian: You're a matchmaker. Was that your question for me? Were you going to try to match me again?

Me: No. I wasn't going to match you!

Christian: Ok. Good. I'm happy with my first match.

Me: Oh, really? What's she like?

Christian: Big attitude, and is very sarcastic.

Christian: But she's gorgeous.

Christian: Have you heard of Rapunzel?

Me: I don't live in a Rapunzel tower!

Christian: Until they fix your elevator, you'd be better off growing your hair out.

Me: Funny.

Christian: What's your ideal match?

I think back to when I randomly filled out my own match questionnaire a few days earlier. It wasn't hard for me to select things. I want all of the things most women want.

Me: Family centered.

I barely press send, and it hits me that I don't think I've ever met a man more family centered than Christian. Other than my dad. Christian has his sister's back a hundred percent, and now he's clearly put his own business on hold for his grandma.

Me: Good sense of humor.

When I press send, I check another box. I've laughed so much with Christian over these cute text messages.

Me: Has a good heart, doesn't take love for granted.

A tear pops into the corner of my eye, and I can't help but get emotional. He hasn't replied while I sent off all these texts, but he must know he meets all the specs, and I'm setting him up.

Me: What about you? What's your perfect match?

I watch my phone screen, now fully awake and I hold my breath waiting for him to flirt. He doesn't reply, and after ten minutes, I risk another text.

Me: Let me guess, needs a working elevator.

I bite my lip, holding back a giggle, and press send. Within seconds, I see he receives my messages and is typing back.

Then he stops typing, and I wait.

I decide to tease him.

Me: I'm ready to ask my question.

He doesn't reply.

THIRTY

Christian

Three days later

"Do you need help with those boxes?" I ask El as she retrieves another large box from the stack of boxes pressed against grandma's bedroom wall.

"Sure. Help me load them in Tom's truck. He left it parked outside. We're donating all this stuff she won't need at the nursing home to Goodwill."

"Tom," I echo, while I grab two boxes and lead the way down the hall. "Do we finally have a name for the mystery man you've been seeing every night?"

"I guess so."

"I confess I already had a name but it's good you've finally told me about him." I push the back door open with my shoulder, holding it while waiting for her to pass through it. "Why all the secret meetups?"

"I was wondering the same thing." She walks in front of me, heading to the curb where the now familiar blue pickup is parked. "I had suspected he was married, but he always denied it. It turns out that he's a first-year lawyer at the same office handling Grandma's estate, and he was assigned to her team. I didn't even know he is a lawyer. When I met him, he was driving an Uber, and he didn't tell me right away. Uber is a side hustle he works to help pay off his school loans.

He didn't realize the conflict of interest until after we already had a couple of dates, and by then he was catching feelings for me. He didn't want me to think he was dating me to get access to grandma's inheritance, nor did he want to get in trouble at work for a conflict of interest. He broke up with me right when he found out, but he never told me why because of client confidentiality. That was when I left school." Reaching the truck, she drops her box into the back and brushes her hands off by rubbing them together.

"Interesting." I plop my box next to hers and push them both back to make room for more.

"We spent the last week talking." Her eyes sparkle back at me, giving away her true feelings about him. "He asked to be transferred to another work team. His boss didn't even care because he understood the accident, and we both want to try to work things out."

I stuff my hands in my pockets and rock back on my heels, enjoying the confession. "You know, I'm going to have to meet his guy before I approve."

"I know. But hey," she pivots and starts walking toward the house, "at least you don't have to worry about supporting me in New York anymore."

"I don't know if that's a huge bonus or not. I'm used to you being there. Now that Portia's back, I have the funds to start looking for an apartment. I envisioned you tagging along."

"I'll still come to visit." She reaches the door first, pulls it open, and we both go inside, grabbing the last of the boxes.

We loop back down the hall and out the backdoor again in silence. I can't think of something to say worthy of the gift that I've been given. I'm so immensely grateful for the chat I had with grandma, and the time I got to spend with her this week. Then miraculously she sprang back to life, even getting to her feet on her own. That is the biggest gift.

Everyone, including Grandma, agreed she'd be safer in a retirement home. We found one not that far away, and it is perfect. Each resident gets their own suite, and they have plenty of activities. When El requested they add Candy Crush tournaments to their rotation of fun, and they agreed, we knew it to be the perfect one. So here we are, loading the last boxes in the truck, and I slam the dented tailgate shut.

It's funny how things are the same for days, and sometimes years, and then one single moment makes your whole world change.

Having my grandma's forgiveness is one of those moments. It seemed to heal the part of my heart that was damaged after my mom died. Everything feels different now. Like I could do anything or go anywhere, and everything would work out.

And there is only one place I want to go.

THIRTY-ONE

Portia

It's been a whole day of working from open to close, and I'm exhausted as I drag my feet up the final staircase to my apartment. I bend over to catch my breath while fumbling for my keys from my purse. I'm about to start watching YouTube videos on how to fix an elevator to handyman ours back to working order. I cannot do ten flights of stairs after working all day on my feet.

My phone vibrates and I pull it out of my pocket as I head down the hall to my apartment. I haven't heard from Christian in days, and my smile can't be contained when I see his name.

Christian: Sorry I've been MIA. My grandma recovered. It's seriously a miracle. We've been busy

cleaning her house because she's moving to a retirement home.

My heart fills with joy for him in all the ways I didn't know it was even attached to him.

Me: That's great news!

Christian: It is. How are you?

Me: OK. The store is good.

Christian: That's good.

Christian: I found out who the mystery man is.

Me: I told you, he's Tom.

Chirstian: I know, but El finally told me.

Christian: He's not married BTW.

Me: Why was he being so secretive?

Christian: I guess he was worried because he is working for grandma's lawyer.

Me: Interesting.

Christian: It is. But not as interesting as something else.

Me: What?

Christian: Whatever your question is.

I sputter out a laugh, as I don't think my original question is worth this much hype. Now that we are a week into this, the pressure's on not to disappoint.

Me: I forgot it.

Christian. Funny.

Christian: Can I ask you a question?

Me: Yeah.

I unlock my door. My shoulders literally decompress the stress of the day as soon as I enter my apartment. It's so good to be home. I shut the door behind me, toss my purse on the chair, and throw my whole body on my bed and read my text.

Christian: Do you want to go somewhere with me tonight?

Me: Tonight? Are you back in town?

Christian: I will be there in about an hour. I'll open the store tomorrow, so you can have the day off and not have to worry about being tired.

Me: Where?

Christian: Secret.

Me: Sure. Just text me when you get here, and I'll come down.

I pin my lips together, suppressing a squeal. Bubbles of excitement rush to my gut, and I feel the jitters all the way to my fingers. One more text bleeps on my phone.

Christian: BTW – I never replied to your question about my perfect match.

Christian: It's you.

THIRTY-TWO

Christian

"You're taking me to work?" Portia's brows rocket north as she stares forward while I park. "I worked sixty hours last week, pulling all the shifts myself. There's no way I'm going back in there." She grabs the dashboard with one hand and secures the door handle in her other, ready to fight an exit from my car.

"Relax." I shut off the engine and open my door, calling back while I meander to my trunk and yank out a heavy duffle bag. "You aren't working. Since it's too late to go anywhere, and El's currently sacked out snoring in our hotel room, I thought we could hang out here."

I honestly don't care where we go. I'd camp in this parking lot in the freezing cold if it meant I got to see her. Her presence offers a balance I desperately need.

"As long as I don't have to make our drinks, I'll come." She drags her feet out of the car, but I have a hunch she's pretending. It's her sarcastic sense of humor I enjoy so much. I'm already fighting back a laugh as I unlock the door and turn on only one set of lights, keeping the place dim.

I set my bag on a nearby table and unzip it. "We don't even need to have coffee. I thought we could make popcorn and watch a movie."

"For real?"

I lift out a projector I'd confiscated from my grandma's basement. It's old and clucky, but it comes with an air of nostalgia. I stack several old black and white film strips next to it. "This should work well if we set it here and aim it at that wall." I position it perfectly, sliding it almost to the edge of a table. "We can either sit in one of these back booths, or I can move them out of the way to sit on the floor." I pause, checking her expression, praying she'll accept this offering. "Unless you hate this idea, we can go back on the dating app to chat."

"Stop it." She playfully punches my arm. "No more dating apps." Her gaze drifts to the row of tables and back to the floor. "This is perfect. I love this idea." She plops down on the floor, stretching her legs out in front of her.

"I hoped you would." I plug in the projector and place a reel on. It's been years since I had a peek at any of these movies. "It's not a romcom," I warn, as I feed the strip through the projector. "It's romance without words. These were my grandma's favorite." I thread the film, flip the switch on the projector, and light flashes on the wall. "And really, the dialogue in romance movies is too cheesy, anyway. They are better without words."

She tips her head back and laughs, showing me her best smile. I pause, watching her. It's funny how this seems so normal. Even though this is technically a first date for us, neither of us seems nervous. "Okay." I clamp my hands together. "I'm going to throw some popcorn in the microwave. What would you like to drink? If you say French press coffee, you die."

She chuckles another full laugh. "I'm telling you; you need to try it. It's superior."

"I have no intention of ever betraying my franchise like that."

"Water is fine."

"Deal." I run back behind the bar to make our snacks all the while I can't stop smiling. "Can I have my question now?" I ask on my return.

"I forgot it." She locks her gaze forward, avoiding me.

"You seriously are a bad liar." I hand her a bowl of fresh popcorn and her drink and then plop down beside her.

"It's lame, and not worth all this hype." She grabs a few kernels out of her bowl and drops them into her mouth one by one.

"Tell me. It can't be worse than any of the other embarrassing stuff you've done in front of me."

"Okay." She sighs, shaking her head. "But don't laugh." Drawing in her legs, she crosses them in front of her and turns toward me. "I must put it into context that I asked you right after we went to the fundraiser. That was before the last week of texting constantly."

"Right." I dig into my bowl and shovel a handful of popcorn into my mouth. I'm famished as I drove straight through all night without stopping because I couldn't wait to see her.

"I was going to ask if you had felt the chemistry I did." Her cheeks blush. She doesn't take her eyes off of me. "I assume since we're both sitting in the Coffee Loft hours after close, getting ready to watch a movie, you felt something."

If she only knew. She's all I've thought about, and I couldn't wait for a chance to tell her this. I haven't stopped thinking about how she felt in my arms when we danced, and how stupid I was that I didn't kiss her.

I can't tell her that though!

I'm determined to make her like me, I put on my best flirty smile. "I would say your assumption is correct."

"Good." Her smile colors my heart neon pink, as it feels as if it's glowing in my chest.

"Shall we watch our movie?" Getting back up on one knee I reach behind me and switch on the projector. The film begins when a lady flashes on the screen. Once I'm happy with the picture alignment, I sit back down and take her hand in mine. We both freeze, sharing a look, before we return our gazes to the screen and watch the movie sitting shoulder to shoulder like this is the most normal thing in the world for us.

My eyes are heavy as tanks when the movie ends. I can barely stay awake. It's been many dreadfully long days in a row, and as much as I want to stay and talk to Portia for hours, my heavy eyelids have another plan. "I'm really sorry to bail on you, but can I take you home now?" I already got off the floor, doing whatever I could not to pass out. "I can barely stay awake, and I have to come back to this place in like four hours."

"Sure." She rises to her feet, standing so close to me, I can smell her. She smells like every summer sunset I've ever watched, and it warms my skin to be near her.

I take a few minutes to pack away the projector, so I don't have to mess with it in the morning. When I return from stowing it in my office, I take her hand in mine again, and we walk together to my car in silence. It's the most comfortable silence I've ever had. Even though we aren't speaking, it's a moment that feels we are creating a bond.

I drive home, the music plays quietly on the radio, and my mind drifts over all the events of the week. Everything from my grandma, to El, to my money issues, and back to land on Portia. It's been one giant roller coaster.

I don't doubt I'm exactly where I need to be.

I park and drop a giant sigh. "I'll walk you up the stairs."

"No, you look exhausted." She waves her hand dismissively at me. "You don't have to. Trust me, I don't even want to walk up them again."

"No, I insist. This is our first date, and I'm all about doing things properly." I open my car door, running to open hers before she can, and we link hands while strolling toward her building.

"I feel like this is boot camp," I joke as we embark on the first set of stairs. I know if I want to do any talking, it's best to get it out now, because I'm going to be out of breath in the next couple of minutes.

She laughs but doesn't reply and we take our time ascending the stairs together. We reach the last landing, and I'm breathing heavily as I walk her straight to her door. She places the key inside, unlocks the door, and pauses, turning back to me. "Thanks for the sweet movie. I'm glad you asked me to go out."

"Ah. You're welcome." This is it. This is where we share our first kiss. Her eyes lock on me, and she doesn't even try to go inside her apartment. I'm so ready for this moment. I've been ready for this moment since the fundraiser.

Something doesn't feel right!

It's not that I'm exhausted. At this moment adrenaline is pumping through my veins, and I'm fully alive. It's that

I know in my heart Portia is special. She will be that girl who consumes me, and suddenly I don't feel enough.

What do I really have to offer her?

I'm practically homeless and barely have a functional business. The customers I do have are all thanks to her. I honestly have not even kissed a woman in well over a year.

Man, I want this to be so special because she's amazing, but I really don't think this is good enough for her.

Instead of leaning in, I chicken out, stuff my hands in my pocket, and smile. "Can I take you to lunch tomorrow?"

"Can you get away from work?"

"Yeah, El came back with me to help out until I get people hired. She said she would come in at noon."

"Sure." Her lashes lower, and she stares at my lips. I can't do this anymore. The look she is giving me is making me weak, and I hold my hand up and wave. "Alright, night!"

"Oh." She straightens her posture, turning toward her door. "Okay. Night."

I spin on my heel and turn before I change my mind. My adrenaline's pumping so hard that I make it down all ten flights of steps in record time. I'm all the way in my car before my phone pings with a text.

Portia: You should have kissed me.

"I know!" I yell loudly inside my car, resisting the urge to chuck my phone. *I'm so mad at myself!* I've been ready for days to kiss her. That's all I think about, but I choked.

Clenching my teeth, I slowly inhale the biggest breath of my life and pull my shoulders back.

I will *not* be that guy who chokes in the last inning.

I must go back up there!

Ten flights of stairs or a thousand—it doesn't matter.

That's my girl, and there's no way I'm going to leave this place with her being disappointed in me!

I yank on my car door handle and set off. My feet fly forward, adrenaline moves them swiftly up the stairs and I practically fly up each new flight. I'm on a mission, and nothing will stop me now.

Sure, I'm breathing heavily, but I've never felt more alive as I charge up the last flight and practically dive the last steps to land with both palms on her door.

This is it.

Pulling out my phone, I construct a text and press send.

Christian: I forgot something. I'm outside your door.

It's eerily quiet as I wait in silence. The long fluorescent hall light flickers behind me.

Portia's door opens slowly. The cute tip of her nose peeks through the crack, but it doesn't take more than a moment for her to open the door wider. She's wearing fuzzy cloud pajamas. She's got a faint trace of mascara smudges under her eyes, but she's never looked more beautiful with the rosy glow on her cheeks. Her brow furrows into concern, and her lips part.

Before she can ask why I'm here, I swoop in, placing one hand on her hip and pull her close to me. My knees buckle, but I don't wimp out as I take her chin in my other hand and guide her mouth toward mine.

Her eyes are wide, but she is not hesitant. I lean closer, inhaling her breath into mine. Her sweet as honey essence wafts under my nose as I inch closer.

I can't bear to close my eyes.

She's so irrationally beautiful.

All I want to do is absorb everything about this moment with all my senses.

Her eyelids close before our lips meet into a sweet, pillowy kiss that leaves the softest tickle under my nose. I seal our kiss with a softer kiss and pull back.

Blinking several times to be sure this was real, my smile only grows larger when she doesn't dither. She stays in my arms, her cheeks glowing. I drop my forehead to touch hers, enjoying having her in my arms. "I've been waiting to do that for so long."

"Me too," she whispers. "You do realize you have to wake up in three hours, don't you?"

Sighing, I know she's right. "Yeah, I need to go, but we're still on for lunch tomorrow, right?"

"Absolutely." Her smile grows, and I take that as an invitation to lean in, stealing another quick smooch.

As I back away, I wave, and softly call, "Good night."

Then I practically float down the stairs, knowing full well there is no way I'm getting any sleep tonight.

But it is worth it.

THIRTY-THREE

Portia

It's noon, and I finally venture out of my apartment after sleeping in all morning. Christian had called when Arielle arrived to relieve him for her shift. He asked me to meet him for lunch. I lock my door, and I'm about to pivot on my heel when my phone dings in my hand.

Christian: Pizza okay, or do you want tacos?

Me: How about we meet at the park and find a food truck? I've been inside all day.

Christian: That sounds amazing.

Christian: Do you want to know something else amazing?

I bat my eyelashes, a blush heating my cheeks as I get ready for him to flirt.

A ping I hadn't heard in months sounds from across the hall at the same time my phone lights up with a text.

Christian: They fixed your elevator.

My insides freeze and I look up as the elevator door opens again. Christian's standing in the middle, phone in one hand, and a sideways grin on his face. "Isn't it amazing that it works?"

"What are you doing here?" I rush inside the elevator, excitement budding in my chest.

He pretends to scoff. "Did you think I could climb those tower stairs again?"

"I thought we were meeting at the park."

"We have a lunch date, and." He takes a step closer to me. "I still need to make up for the other time I didn't kiss you." His hand drops to my hip, and his eyes pace between my eyes and lips. I know this look. I've memorized it by now, and I am so ready to kiss him.

As if on cue, the elevator door closes, and music plays out of the speakers, a light jazz that couldn't set the mood better if I had tried. As he leans in, he doesn't close his eyes. My eyelids drift down as our lips meet in the sweetest smooch. My heartrate skyrockets all the while I struggle to prevent my knees from knocking together. I can't help but wonder how I got so lucky.

We ride the elevator down with our lips locked until the door dings, and rapidly opens. Startling us to take a step back, we both stare wide-eyed. My jaw drops. Mrs. Nelson is walking Oliver, and they are waiting for the elevator on the bottom floor. "Who let you guys out?"

She waddles inside, taking her time, but Oliver's a good companion not pulling her faster than she can manage. "We walked to the mailbox because it's such a lovely day out."

"I see that." A smile spreads across my face as Oliver greets me by licking my hands. "Hey, boy. I'm sorry I didn't walk you today."

"He's fine." She pats his head and takes a step toward the door. "I'd better hurry back upstairs before the elevator breaks again and traps me down here."

I nervously chuckle, not at all doubting that could happen. Mrs. Nelson looks back at me. "Well, I'm afraid I do have bad news, and I hope it doesn't upset you. I do think now that I don't have to take the stairs, I'll be able to walk Oliver all the time. I enjoy getting outside."

I bite back a smile, not wanting her to see that I consider this good news. "I will miss our walks, but I totally understand. I'm getting regular shifts at the Coffee Loft again, and my website will be just fine." I bravely reach out, grab Christian's hand, and lace my fingers through his. We step out of the elevator together as I call back, "Besides, I don't need to look for hunks anymore. *I just had my last first date.* "

Epilogue

Six months later

"Well." Christian brushes his hands together and swipes the newly signed contract off the desk. "That settles it." Slipping the contract into a manilla envelope, he seals it all the while his eyes are on me. "A business partner is the last thing I ever wanted, as I had dreams of building this empire by myself, but I can't afford not to keep you around."

"It's hard to believe we ended up as partners after the rocky start we had." I chuckle reminiscently as I stand, and we both exit Christian's Coffee Loft office together. It's Friday night, after closing and we're the only ones in the store.

"I guess you're no longer my boss." My lips curl into a dubious grin. "We are now equals, which means I get to make decisions, too."

"Oh, man." Christian playfully rolls his eyes. "What did I get myself into?"

Tapping my chin, I pretend to assess the store. "It looks like we might need to do a little remodeling." I walk to the coffee bar and motion to the empty counter space. "We need a long row of French presses here—"

My voice drops off because I find a random French press with a giant gold bow on it, sitting exactly where I had motioned. *How'd that happen?* "What's this doing here?" I motion to it, as it's clearly out of place. I had just cleaned this counter. It must be part of one of his jokes.

"Pardon my French press." Christian swoops in front of me, and slides the press off the counter, removing the lid with his other hand while tipping the canister toward me. "That's because I have a question for you."

"You do?" I ran my tongue over my lips, hydrating them. "What is it?"

A glimmer of light reflects off something inside as my heart slams against my chest, pounding so loudly it echoes in my ears. Everything's playing in slow motion, and I want to scream in all caps that I can't believe this is happening!

"Oh, wait a second. I thought I had a question." Christian mumbles with a taunting grin on his face. "I forgot what it is."

"No, you didn't." I squawk out with a high-pitched laugh.

"Maybe I didn't forget, but it's really late." His gaze slides to the door, and he takes a step back. "I need to get to bed."

"That's pure torture." My stomach tanks, yanking my heart with it. I can't believe he's playing me like this.

"Oh, look." He points to the backroom as his sarcastic grin appears. "The store's on fire."

"I don't like you anymore." Pushing my pouting lip out, I cross both arms in front of my chest and take a giant step toward the door.

"Stop." He holds his hand up. "It's just a joke." He slides in front of me with the ring in his hand. A perfect princess cut on a white gold band. We never talked about rings, but it's exactly what I would have wanted. "After I had the contract drawn up this week, I was thinking about partnerships a lot. It wasn't enough for us to be business partners. I can't imagine my *life* without you. When you know, you know. I want that for us—to be life partners."

His eyes sparkle, and I'm back to screaming in all caps inside as he takes a knee and holds the ring out. "Will you marry me?"

"Yes." I squeeze my toes together as he slides the ring on. I eagerly pucker my lips, but he doesn't kiss me. Instead, he smiles one of his secret smiles at me, signaling my interest to pique. "What's going on?"

"Just one thing?"

Ice runs through my veins, as I can't believe he's placing a condition on our engagement. It's such odd timing, and my brows angle down. "What is it?"

"You have to agree from now and until *forever* the only French presses we are going to have in this store is your lips on mine."

"Deal." I smile sweetly and press my lips on his. While our lips are pressed together, I reach back and grab the French press off the counter. When I pull back from our kiss, I slip on a sly smile and hug my French press to my chest. "This is coming home with me."

Welcome to the Coffee Loft,

where the romance is always brewing.

Grab your favorite table over in the corner and be prepared to be swept off your feet. This multi-author collection features some of your favorite sweet romance authors that you already know and love as well as a few new names you'll be rushing to check out. From cold brews to cappuccinos and frothy frappes, there's something on the menu for every romantic comedy reader. Fake dates, meddling matchmakers, friends-to-lovers and so much more, each stand-alone story is the right blend of sweetness, guaranteed to warm your heart.
Happily-ever-afters coming right up!

Series link →https://books.bookfunnel.com/thecoffee
loftseries
Guess what else? I have another release planned for this
series and it's up for preorder now.
No More Mr. Chai Guy → https://www.amazon.com
/dp/B0CQDQCF8F

KISSED BY MY BILLIONAIRE BOSS
(COMING 2024)

Just one summer in our youth, and the most awkward kiss ever-but it was enough to imprint on my heart *forever*.

One of the most tortuous things a soul can endure is to meet the right person at the *wrong time*.

For me, it was Graham—a quiet, writing recluse with eyes colored like my mother's sapphire ring.

I was the cliché.

Just a girl-next-door, a little too-young with too much spunk. Not to mention, the queen of the wardrobe malfunctions. I was obviously annoying to him. Somewhere along the way, he learned to tolerate me.

Maybe.

Or was that just what I told myself?

Through Graham, life taught me that it's often cruel and unfair. Sometimes you're the one who ends up with a broken heart. I tried to move on, but I never forgot my boy with sapphire eyes. Then, one day, he stumbled back into my life.

Only this time, he was the guy who signs my paycheck.

Find out what happened when the boy who stole my heart grew up and unexpectedly becomes my boss.

Kissed by my Billionaire Boss is a clean and wholesome, second chance, friends to lovers, sweet romance with heart and comedy.

Genre: Clean and Sweet Romcoms.

Also By J.P. Sterling

***Bosses and Billionaires Series* (All Standalones)**

Maid for my Billionaire Boss

Upcycling My Rig-Pig Boss

Marooned with My Celebrity Boss (Coming 2024)

Kissed by My Billionaire Boss (Coming April 2024)

A Heart that Dances Series

Dancing on Broken Ankles

The Stars We See

A Heart that Dances

A Heart that Loves

Water and Stone Duet

Ruby in the Water

Lily in the Stone

<u>Christmas Shenanigans (All Standalones)</u>
Mingle All the Way
Tis the Season to Get Married
<u>The Coffee Loft Series (All Standalones)</u>
Pardon My French Press
No More Mr. Chia Guy (Coming Fall 2024)

About J.P. Sterling

Hey you! Thanks for being here.

Let me introduce myself.

I write wholesome stories and adore all things slapstick humor and heart strings.

Growing up, I binged on classic comedy like Lucille Ball, and Carol Burnette. It was a great escape from reality, even when the plots were farfetched. I discovered my love for writing slapstick comedy after motherhood, and I haven't looked back.

Aside from writing, I'm also a wife and homeschooling mom, a holistic nutritionist, a jewelry designer, a professional archivist, former college instructor and lover of all things dark chocolate.

Author Clean Code: I like to make my stories about the story and not about a bunch of profanity, mature content, or graphic violence that are only there to shock you. I write my stories to be family friendly.

Let's get social!

I just launched a private reader group on Facebook. I can't wait to welcome you there. This is where we share all the things humor and heartstrings.

Hop in my reader group here: →**https://www.faceb ook.com/groups/1500850764081965**

FREE AUDIO BOOKS: → **https://www.youtube. com/c/JpSterling**

INSTAGRAM: →*https://www.instagram.com/au thorjpsterling/*

FREE NEWSLETTER: →**https://landing.mailerli te.com/webforms/landing/q9c0v3**

FACEBOOK PAGE: → **https://www.facebook.co m/jpsterlingauthor/**

www.ingramcontent.com/pod-product-compliance
Lightning Source LLC
Chambersburg PA
CBHW061248310726
48971CB00007B/2270